TOO MANY YESTERDAYS

Debra Langford flees to Bamburra Island, off the Australian mainland, to recapture her artistic talents, following a painful broken romance. There she falls under the spell of the island's mysterious Luke Darcy, who appears to have no past and no family. Sorely tempted to trust a man about whom she knows almost nothing, she is forced to ignore what her heart tells her when she learns Luke has a visitor — a beautiful woman — and his past starts to catch up with him.

Books by Jo James
in the Linford Romance Library:

CHANCE ENCOUNTER
THE RELUCTANT BACHELOR
SHADOWS ACROSS THE WATER
SECRET OF THE RIDGE
AN UNEASY ARRANGEMENT
MYSTERY AT BLUFF COTTAGE
IMPETUOUS HEART

JO JAMES

TOO MANY YESTERDAYS

Complete and Unabridged

LINFORD
Leicester

First published in Great Britain in 2004

First Linford Edition
published 2005

British Library CIP Data

James, Jo,
   Too many yesterdays.—Large print ed.—
Linford romance library
1. Love stories
2. Large type books
I. Title
823.9'2 [F]

ISBN 1–84395–701–9

Published by
F. A. Thorpe (Publishing)
Anstey, Leicestershire

Set by Words & Graphics Ltd.
Anstey, Leicestershire
Printed and bound in Great Britain by
T. J. International Ltd., Padstow, Cornwall

This book is printed on acid-free paper

1

A frisson of expectation scudded up Debra Langford's spine. She was starting over, having made the bold decision to go for a life totally different from the disastrous one she was leaving behind. Forgetting the yesterdays wasn't going to be easy, but hey, she'd find the strength to make the tomorrows promising.

Bamburra Island, here I come, she thought.

As the ferry docked, she struggled with an overwhelming desire to rush headlong down the stairs to retrieve her car and be on her way. But the vehicles were parked below in order of arrival, and she'd been quite late in boarding. Besides, why hurry? Enjoy the experience, she told herself, you have your accommodation booked for tonight at Koala Bay.

Lovely name . . . lovely thought.

Wow! Three months on the island to recapture her zest for life and her ability to sketch.

There were very few vehicles left in the ferry's parking hold when she arrived, and the slight chaos of cars driving off was all but over.

As she eased her hatchback towards the ferry's gaping mouth on to dry land, glancing beyond, she saw that the road forked to the left at the top of the hill. Even more noticeable was the tall, broad-shouldered man who'd captured her interest earlier on the bow of the ferry, securing the mooring ropes with strong, muscled arms. He stood by the exit, directing the last of the drivers off. Again she admired his body, and found herself indulging in thoughts of gyms and work-outs.

Tossing back her shoulders, she reminded herself she'd sworn off men because right now she was in danger of falling at the first hurdle. Still, a girl could wonder. And having convinced herself of that, idling the motor, she wound down her window and said brightly, 'Excuse me, but which road do I take to Koala Bay?'

'Ignore the first on the left. Go straight ahead.'

She waited for his smile, expecting it to be welcoming, but his dark eyes, his deep voice vaguely suggested . . . was it boredom?

Well, wouldn't he be bored? He probably answered the same question time after time.

Glancing behind to reassure herself she wasn't holding up the few cars remaining, she said, 'Thanks. I wasn't expecting it to get dark so soon. I hope the road's well lit.'

Luke tried not to sound irritated, after all, he no longer sat in a modern office with other people to do the leg work for him. Now he was paid to keep the customers happy, not run the show. He tried to sound enthusiastic.

'You're on a great little piece of God's earth, but it's sparsely populated, and it doesn't come with advertising

3

signs. That's its attraction to visitors.'

Did her eyes turn a little wary, her lips quiver, or did he simply notice she had wide eyes and full, unpainted lips?

'I think you're going to tell me there are twists and turns, too.'

'Just a few.'

'How long will it take? Ten, fifteen minutes?'

He reached his arms across to the roof of her car and leaned closer.

'I thought you said you were going to Koala Bay.'

'Yes, but . . . hey, I'm starting to feel bad vibes here. Is there another problem?'

Ah, he thought, she's one of those impetuous women who comes over on a whim and arrives totally unprepared.

'Unfortunately, there is. Koala Bay is a fifty-minute drive from here.'

She laughed.

'Oh, please, would you stop winding me up?'

He straightened and smiled.

'There is some good news. The roads are signposted.'

She hit her forehead with the palm of her hand. Her long dark hair flounced across her shoulders, covering part of her cheek.

'I can't believe this.'

'Look, I have to help tie up the Sea Star, but if you care to hang around I can . . . '

'What? I hope you're not going to suggest I stay over at your place,' she said quickly.

He could understand her being upset but, damn it, her response really tested his already brittle patience.

'I'm going to do you a favour and forget you said that.'

She brushed her long hair away from her face.

'I'm feeling a bit scratchy. To be honest, I'm having a problem processing what you're telling me.'

'OK.'

He folded his arms across his chest, determined to make it unambiguously clear the position she was in.

'Here's the situation. It's getting

dark. You've got a fifty-minute journey ahead of you and the roads are narrow and twisting. You'll need to drive carefully because the kangaroos come on to the roads at night without warning. If you're travelling too fast . . . '

She groaned.

'I assumed the ferry berthed at the largest town, and now you're telling me it doesn't.'

Just as he thought. She's a bit scatty, likes her own way and isn't coping well with the onset of a bad mood, but on the plus side, she had sensational luminous pale blue eyes which glinted with irritation in the rapidly descending darkness. Hopefully she had a sense of humour hidden beneath her present flush of annoyance. He smiled, tried to unearth at least a glimpse of it.

'We're in Iluka, where the ferry docks. You're not the first person to make the mistake. Think of it this way. You'll get to know the island more quickly on the drive, and you'll have a good after-dinner yarn when you get home.'

The sensational blue eyes glowered.

'If I get back. I was advised to stay at Koala Bay, but no-one bothered to tell me it was miles from here. Stupid me. I thought people in the tourist industry were supposed to be helpful. Seems I got that wrong, too.'

He wanted to remind her of her responsibilities when she arranged the trip, but a car horn behind them sounded. She jumped and suddenly he felt a kind of a responsibility for her dilemma. Uncomfortable, he raked a hand through his hair.

'You'll have to move on now, but if you pull off to the side of the road halfway up the hill and wait until I finish here, you can follow me to Koala Bay. I live there.'

'Thanks, but by the time I wait for you I could be halfway there. Perhaps I'll run into you some time,' she said, shoving the gear lever into drive, and taking off, her hair streaming behind her in the breeze through the open window.

He lifted his shoulders. Pity, she's probably going to regret it, he thought. And smiling, he made his way back to the passenger lounge of the Sea Star. There was something about her which appealed to him. Lovely eyes, sure, prickly certainly, but he'd met plenty of women with at least one of those attributes, often both. So what made her stand out, he puzzled.

Deb's car bumped over the landing ramp on to the road. She accelerated up the hill, castigating herself for allowing her anxiety to override her commonsense. It wasn't the man in the blue shirt's fault she hadn't done her homework before she took this journey. It was her anxiety to get away from the city. In hindsight, he'd been fairly patient with her, even offered some help. But it was too late to go back and say, yes, I'll stick around and wait for you, especially as she'd determined after her break-up with Guy that she'd swallowed enough humble pie from men to last a lifetime.

She wound up the window of the car with a swift, jerky movement and kept driving.

Beyond the terminus lights, darkness seemed to engulf her. Her hatchback crept along, until finally, on a distant hill, the tail-lights of a car glowed like tiny red stars, sparking hope in her tense body. She accelerated, using its lights as a guide, but within minutes, she'd lost it in the twists and turns and was again driving into a shroud of darkness. Only the white strip running up the centre of the road in her full-beam lights offered a glimmer of reassurance which, in her state of apprehension, was so minimal as to be practically useless.

She pulled to the edge of the road, took a few deep breaths, tried to think clearly. Perhaps she could stay overnight in Iluka and go into Koala Bay tomorrow? But that meant turning back to the road fork, and searching in the dark for somewhere to stay in an unknown little village when she could be making ground to her destination. It also meant phoning the place she'd booked to inform them not to expect her tonight, and paying for a night she didn't use. It wouldn't break her, but she was operating on a tight budget, having planned to function for three months without a regular income.

Dragging a bottle of water from her backpack, she took a long drink. Her eyes began to adjust to the darkness. The lights of an approaching car flashed into her rear view mirror. She set down her bottle and prepared to follow it. The car whipped by. Her man in the blue shirt, she wondered. Quickly she pulled on to the road and tracked behind it, relying on its tail-lights to guide her. Now, all she had to do was keep up with it.

Breathing more easily, her foot heavy on the accelerator, the speedometer climbed dangerously, her heart beating wildly. She eased back and gradually the car ahead disappeared altogether. She was driving along a lonely thin black reptile with a white line down its back threatening her at every turn, and seemingly stretching into for ever. She became a shaky, sweaty mess.

The car crawled endlessly into the night, as she paid out on herself for not being practical and taking up the offer of the man in the blue shirt. Of course she didn't take it up. He was a man. So what? Surely she could have overlooked that this one time. He wasn't asking anything of her.

'Huh,' she said aloud, as if to emphasise the point, 'he's a man. He'd probably have worked around to it.'

And yet, he'd seemed genuinely aggrieved when she anticipated his offer of help back at the terminal.

She jabbed at the radio button, hoping to drown out her ridiculous thoughts. He hadn't shown the vaguest interest in her. She could have had two heads or horns for all the notice he took. Perhaps that's what miffed her. She'd certainly noticed him — the broad shoulders, the tanned, muscled arms, the crop of dark hair, slightly longer than fashionable, and darkish blue eyes which, it occurred to her now, had a faraway expression.

He was probably discontented with his job. Probably thought he was too handsome to be doing service work and hoped he'd be discovered by some magazine or film production company. Listing the possibilities occupied her mind, but try as she did, she couldn't find much about him to disapprove, except his gender.

Radio static cut into her meanderings. Well, what did she expect? The island probably closed down, like some ancient, walled settlement, after the church bells announced, 'Six o'clock and all is well.'

She began to feel cold and wished she'd worn jeans and a sweater instead of the cropped holiday pants and cotton top. Perhaps she should stop and put on her coat, but it looked pretty dark and lonely, and suppose some wild animal was lurking in the bushes? It would be easier to turn off the radio and activate the heater.

The sudden stillness spooked her. She decided to sing, but what? As a child, on motoring holidays with her grandparents, they used to sing hackneyed old songs. She'd scoffed and said, 'They're really gross, Gran,' and giggled. Incredibly the words and the tunes stuck and now she found herself singing, 'Pack up your troubles . . . ', smiling at the irony of it.

A green signpost loomed ahead in the high beam. She'd simply have to stop now. If she took the wrong turn . . . She groaned as she pulled to the side of the road and saw that the road on the left turned off to a place called Amaroo. Did you go through Amaroo to get to Koala Bay? Dear heaven, if only she'd brought a map of the island.

Another car was approaching. Her heart leaped. How to signal it to stop?

Press down her horn and let it rip? It flashed by so she pulled on to the road behind it and followed beyond the turn to Amaroo, judging that as Koala Bay was the main town it would be the destination of most cars.

She eased back her shoulders. This time she wouldn't lose her source of light. It was her only confirmation that other human beings existed. Her foot leaned on the accelerator and she kept pace, making good progress, until up ahead, hopping on to the road, came not one but three kangaroos!

She screamed, her foot hitting the brake. She felt a slight bump as the car skidded to a halt. The last kangaroo stood as if mesmerised by her lights.

'Heavens, I've hit the stupid thing. I can't believe the night I'm having.'

Trying not to make a noise, she slipped out of the car but the animal took a giant leap and went crashing into the bushes.

Now what? Did she go looking for it in case she'd injured it, or what? She glanced into the heavy vegetation, shivering. No way dare she venture into the bush. In the dark she could tread on a snake, trip over a wombat swaggering through the undergrowth or break her ankle. Besides, her legs wouldn't make it, even if her heart hadn't already decided to wave the white flag.

'Come on, come on,' she cried into the night, jumping when a dingo howled in response.

'Please, someone, anyone, help me.'

A flash of light hit the bitumen and soon a vehicle came into view, its lights raking across the area where she stood. She let out a long breath. If she went into the centre of the road and signalled it down, would it run her over? A more horrible thought slithered into her mind. Suppose it stopped and a modern-day Jack the Ripper stepped from it? She'd take her chance, equip herself with the manicure scissors she kept in the car's glove compartment. Anything was better than being alone out here.

In contrast with her heartbeat, the car slowed, and shuddered to a stop behind her. Clutching the small scissors, she raced to it, and beat on the driver's seat window of the off-road vehicle. The driver began to wind down the window.

'What's your problem? Had an accident?'

She nodded vigorously.

'I think I may have run . . . I mean injured a kangaroo,' she said and then her voice fell. 'Oh, it's you.'

Just when she thought her dreadful night was about to end, the man in the blue shirt opened the door and stepped easily from the vehicle. She hated to admit it, even to herself, but waves of relief washed through her, as he said, 'Hello to you, too. We have to stop meeting like this.'

If she could see his eyes she'd know if he was joking or mocking her, but the evening light told her only that he was tall and strong, certainly not menacing. She decided not to say anything which might give him an excuse to abandon her.

'Yes, we should,' she muttered, rather stuck for a satisfactory response.

'But since I'm here, where's this 'roo you've run down? I thought I warned you not to drive too fast.'

'I was trying to stay with a car ahead of me.'

He shrugged.

'It's too late now. Did you think to look inside the poor creature's pouch to see if it had a young one?'

'I don't even know if I hit it. I felt a bump, the silly thing stood looking at me, I braked, got out of the car and it ran off into the bushes.'

'The headlights stupefy them for a bit. And, by the way, on Bamburra Island, our kangaroos don't run, they hop.'

She forced a mocking smile. Men couldn't help it. They had to patronise you.

'A slip of the tongue. We all have them.'

Even you, she almost added, before checking herself.

'Shouldn't we be doing something to see if I did any damage?'

'We?'

It cost her, but she sensed his patience had begun to desert him now that he was on his own time, and backed off again.

'OK, what do you suggest?'

'Where did it enter the bush?'

'Here, I think.'

She indicated a spot where a tree had been slightly flattened.

As he strode towards it, he growled, 'Haven't you got a coat or something warm to put on? You'll freeze in this southerly.'

'And you won't? I don't see you wearing one.'

'I'm a man.'

'As if I hadn't noticed. I bet a big, strong man like you doesn't cry either,' she mocked, her irritation on the march again.

'Same answer.'

Put a sock in it or he'll be out of here in a shot, she warned herself. She came as close to apologising as her pride would allow.

'If that's your excuse I accept it, provided you accept mine. I'm anxious and frustrated, and damn it, I feel extremely fragile at the moment. I'd almost given up on someone stopping.'

'Accepted,' he muttered. 'Probably tourists. The locals always stop if they think a motorist's in trouble. These are lonely roads at night.'

'I'd noticed that, too.'

He leaned against the side of the car.

'Any chance you've got a torch stashed in your glove compartment?'

She tilted her head. He'd reminded her again how ill-equipped she was for this journey, and it did nothing for her state of mind. She shook her head.

'I suggest you make it your first purchase when you get to Koala Bay. Nobody on the island goes out at night without a light of some kind.'

He turned, strode to his car, yanked

open the door and was soon back at her side, a powerful torch lighting his way.

'You think the 'roo disappeared about here? If it's been hurt, it won't have gone far.'

Deb shivered again. She should get her coat, but she was anxious about the animal's well-being, and waited, her gaze fixed on the man as he flattened a path into the thick undergrowth with long strides. Soon she could see only a splinter of light, but his cursing, the crashing of footsteps over the rough terrain came back to her on the wind, and brought a smile to her lips.

She took a moment to grab her coat, shrugged into it and tucked her hands into its sleeves. She hadn't realised until he mentioned it how cold the evening had grown. Now the wind seemed to reach into her bones. Her teeth began to chatter.

Given a choice, she'd have preferred someone else had stopped to help, but timing had brought him along. And she felt safe for the first time in what seemed like for ever. Grateful, too? Naturally. But that didn't mean she had to like him.

At last she could hear him charging back. The torchlight preceded him out of the bushes, and he appeared, his dark hair awry, plucking debris from his shirt and trousers.

'Did you find anything?' she demanded.

'Negative.'

'What does that mean?'

'If you hit the animal, it couldn't have done much damage. Kangaroos are tough customers. My guess is its paddock's away from here by now. I'll let the ranger know in the morning to keep a look-out for one slightly damaged kangaroo.'

'Thanks.'

It was totally inadequate, but it would have to do. Perhaps later when she wasn't so cold and miserable she could be more gracious.

'Now, get back into your car, turn on the heater, and wait for me to get in front before you pull out. Then follow me into Koala Bay. Can you do that without any mishaps?'

He shone the torch on his watch.

'Crikey, is it that late?'

Why couldn't he be short and wear glasses and a cardigan? Why couldn't he be a skinny, balding, mean-faced banker? How much easier it would have been to go along with his orders. But, he had the build and good looks of a football idol, and the assumption of superiority to go with them, and she'd come to this island to get away from masterful men who thought they had the authority to tell her what to do. No wonder she rebelled.

'What's the problem? Does your lady get anxious if you're late home?'

'You could say that.'

So he had a woman in his life. What was the matter with her, thinking uncharitable thoughts, behaving like a spiteful teenager? If he took off without her she'd have only herself to blame. She tried to ease her conscience, to smooth over her gaffe by saying quietly, 'It feels like midnight. How late is it anyway?'

'Ten o'clock. I'm Luke Darcy by the way.'

When his tone softened, she felt positively wretched for behaving with such belligerence. If he hadn't stopped, or if he chose to pay her back for her rudeness, she could find herself stranded. She imagined herself limping into town in the early morning, a spaced-out, incoherent mess. She decided to grovel a bit.

'It was good of you to stop and to care about the 'roo ... er, Luke. I'm Debra Langford, but my friends call me Deb.'

When he opened the door for her, in its light, did she notice a cynical rise of his brows? She climbed in, urging herself to ignore her negativity.

'Now, do as you're told and don't move until I'm in front, and then follow,' he ordered.

'Only if you promise not to drive like

a formula one expert.'

'Trust me. I'll make sure you're always within distance.'

He closed her door and she placed her shaky hands on the wheel to still them, wondering if she could actually control the steering wheel.

His horn blasted as he passed her. She started up her engine. The headlights stuttered once, twice, and went out, then the motor grunted several times, but refused to start. Again and again she turned the key, pumped the accelerator, but the sinking feeling in her stomach signalled the futility of it. She'd left the headlights on and the heater running when she got out of the car to see what had happened to the kangaroo!

She glanced up. Luke Darcy's vehicle had disappeared around the bend.

2

Deb's hand pounded the horn. It sounded into the dark. How would she explain this latest disaster to Mr Know-it-all Darcy when he came back? Assuming of course, he did return.

Of course, he'll come back, she reassured herself. He's the kind of man who likes to show off his strength, demonstrate his superiority. He wouldn't leave her stranded. She checked her doors to be sure they were locked and waited, rehearsing what she'd do and say when he did finally return. Nothing must interfere with her goal of reaching Koala Bay tonight. Darcy, she suspected, reacted negatively to women who stood up for themselves, so she was in no position to bargain or to insult him.

Ho hum, she sighed, another man, another put-down.

Later she might look back on her predicament and laugh, but she didn't have even the suggestion of a smile on her lips at the moment. All she had was hope.

It seemed an age before a car's high-beam headlights picked out the road, illuminating the adjoining vegetation as dark, shadowy shapes. She held her breath. She could hear the motor. She could see the car. Her heart began to thump.

It stopped on the other side of the road before reaching her, took two sweeps to turn on the narrow bitumen and skidded to a halt in loose stones in front of her hatchback. She let out a long breath as the door slammed, and his feet thudded into the road's metal as he strode back to her. He was hunched in a padded, windproof jacket, its collar turned up around his neck. He looked big, he looked savage. If she hadn't recognised the vehicle, she might have doubted his identity. The thought of explaining to him made her feel nauseous.

Play it cool, be nice, Deb, she

pleaded with her natural inclination to tell him to get lost. She needed the guy's help to get to Koala Bay. After that she'd wave him goodbye for-ever, which somehow didn't make her feel a whole lot easier as she opened her door and swung her feet out.

'Well, what the devil's holding you up now?' he demanded.

'Er . . . I feel so stupid. The battery's flat,' she said, giving her best imitation of meek and mild.

He muttered something and growled, 'Did you do anything at all to prepare for this trip? Next you're going to run out of petrol.'

'I did buy a ferry ticket.'

She tried to sound cheerful, but it didn't come off.

'You wouldn't have got this far without one.'

Don't let him get to you. Stay nice.

'Do you think you can recharge the battery?'

'I have to get home some time tonight.'

'I forgot. My apologies, your lady's waiting up for you.'

'Collect your overnight things, lock up your car and let's get out of here.'

That really tested her resolve to stay nice.

'Excuse me? I can't leave my car out here in the middle of nowhere. Why can't you use your jump leads to start it?'

'Because I haven't got them with me.'

'Ah! So you're not as well prepared as . . . '

She stopped there, deciding she'd better go back to nursing along his ego. He started to walk away, shrugging off his coat.

'Suit yourself. I'm off.'

She needed no further encouragement to reach for her backpack, lock the doors and hurtle along to catch up with him.

'What if someone vandalises my car overnight and steals my luggage?'

'It'll be OK. You're in more danger should a venomous snake curl up in the warmth under the car and hang around until you get back.'

She shuddered.

'You're joking?'

'I never joke about snakes.'

'OK, so you've frightened me. Happy?'

He tossed his coat into the back of the car and as he took her backpack from her, his hand touched hers. It felt warm, reassuring, and to her surprise, even his voice took on an encouraging tone.

'You'll be fine, Deb. I'll check it out in the morning when we get back to pick up the car.'

He held open her door and as she climbed into his vehicle, her thoughts took wing. She couldn't quibble with his competence, and in situations like this, competence rated. Though it wasn't merely his efficiency that made Luke different from the men she'd had in her life. He had such a confident saunter, a way of raising his dark brows which would unsettle any woman's self-possession.

She stole a glance at him as he settled

into the driver's seat, her heart on the move. If you liked your men dark, he was something else, but once she'd thought Guy wildly handsome, so smart, that she'd overlooked the arrogance. A bright girl only did that once in a lifetime.

As the car accelerated, her body began to thaw, she started to feel alive again, confident she'd make it to Koala Bay tonight, and in one piece, thanks to Luke. She retreated into the soft leather of her seat, weary, prepared to leave the conversation to him, because every time she said something she risked worsening her standing with him.

Luke concentrated on the road. He knew it well, having made the journey to the ferry terminal twice a day for some time, but at night the kangaroos, and other marsupials who emerged from the bush at dusk to enjoy the freedom of the evening light, caused some anxiety. He could feel the warmth of his companion's presence, in fact he wondered if she hadn't brought the suggestion of a delicate fragrance into the car. He tried not to focus on her for his thoughts made him uncomfortable, as did the notion that he may have been too tough on her, too unwelcoming.

On the phone his sister had recently accused him again of intolerance towards her daughter.

'You've never suffered fools gladly. You had plenty of practice at it when you occupied a top job at the bank, but now you're in a different position.'

She'd lowered her voice.

'I know it's been tough on you and I'm trying to understand your frustration, but you must have known, Leigh, that . . . '

'Meg!' he'd shouted into the phone, 'how many times do I have to tell you, it's Luke? I'm known as Luke now.'

'Sorry, I'm still trying to get used to it. Anyway I was saying, you're in the service industry now. Tourists need to be treated with kid gloves, and if you're too bossy, you could blow your job.'

She'd tried to soften the message with a laugh.

'Sometimes I think you've suffered a youth by-pass.'

'Sometimes I think you take too much notice of other people. I'm thirty two, not a retiree.'

Meg had raised him after their parents died in an accident when he was eight and she twenty. She'd given him a loving, but sensible and practical upbringing. Not so her own child. He was fifteen when his sister announced her pregnancy and her plan to bring up the child as a single mother. She'd delivered a daughter, cherished and indulged her.

'Have I said thanks to you recently for raising me?' he'd said, anxious not to be drawn into talking about his niece.

He'd sensed her smile.

'You were a cinch, kid,' she'd said, tunefully.

He'd tried to stay light-hearted.

'Enough of the kid stuff, eh, big sister?'

'Have you lived on the island long?'

He frowned. That wasn't his sister's voice he had heard.

'You were saying?'

'I asked how long you've lived over here.'

Ah, of course, the tetchy Miss, or was it Ms Langford sat beside him.

'Not long,' he said, deliberately evasive.

'Weeks, years?' she persisted.

Being quizzed about the past made him squirm.

'I haven't been counting.'

She tried again.

'You weren't born here?'

'No.'

'What's the big secret?'

Thank goodness she sounded amused.

'No secret. Everyone knows I wasn't born here.'

How could he get her off the subject?

'Are you from Adelaide? I'm from Melbourne.'

He almost said, 'Me, too,' but in time held back the information. She was probably only making conversation, but over the months he'd stuck to his policy not to talk about himself even to strangers.

'Nice city,' he said. 'What brings you to the island? A holiday or something else?'

She shrugged.

'I may stay for a while. It depends on how I settle in. But with the start I've had, I don't think the place likes me.'

Easier now the conversation had switched back to her, he laughed.

'Don't be hard on yourself. You made some very elementary mistakes. Coming here isn't the same as a trip to Sydney. Hopefully you've got all the glitches out of the way at the beginning.'

'I admit I didn't come prepared, but from where I'm standing, I'm not entirely to blame. The island tourist body should lift its game if it expects to keep the visitors coming. Why have a six o'clock evening crossing when the largest town is fifty minutes away? Tourists are bound to get caught in the dark for most of the year.'

What made her so edgy, so ready to argue? Actually she had a lot going for her. He couldn't help noticing her lovely blue eyes back there on the ferry when they flashed with irritation. As for her figure, she looked fit, shapely. Standing beside him, he'd assessed her as not catwalk tall. Perhaps her long hair, the cut-off pants she wore made her appear of model-height, but he couldn't ignore the fact that she had attitude. Not that he objected to women with spirit and opinions, but he did take exception to over-zealous feminists, who looked for a politically incorrect fault in every syllable a man spoke. Odd that he should care, but he hoped she wasn't one.

'It's scheduled for the convenience of the island people who travel to and from the mainland for work, and for day-trippers. Why didn't you book on the morning run?'

'It was full.'

'And you couldn't wait,' he said lightly.

He'd decided he wouldn't win any verbal joust with Ms Langford in her present tetchy state. She was obviously tired, over-anxious, frustrated — a woman used to having things fall into place rather than organising them that way. He was the opposite. Once he'd had a very organised life, knew where he wanted to go, how to get to the top of his profession, and had made giant strides.

He still rated the ability to organise as a big plus. But it no longer featured in the top ten of his must haves. When his life collapsed suddenly, society spat him out like lava from an erupting volcano, and in search of a way ahead, he'd found the island. Sure, his organising skills had helped him regain some momentum, but now he relied entirely on his own resources, never on anyone else to do his bidding.

'What made you decide to come to Bamburra on your own?' he asked into an uncomfortable silence.

'I wanted peace, space, time to chill

out, I guess. I'm a graphic artist with a yen to paint.'

The single city girls he'd known hadn't taken holidays to find peace and space. They'd sought sea, sunshine and night life along the mecca of developed resorts dotting Australia's coastline. She'd opted for the solitude of a small island, still undeveloped, which attracted nature lovers and families to its shores. Vaguely he wondered if she, too, was escaping from the real world.

'Oil painting?' he asked. 'I'm trying my hand at sketching.'

'Oh.'

She sounded disinterested.

'I'm into water colours mainly.'

'You couldn't have come to a better spot for inspiration. But you might be lonely. Is it Ms or Mrs Langford?'

Damn it, what prompted such a personal question?

She moved restlessly in her seat, then said rather sharply, 'Ms will do. How much longer before we get there?'

Her terse reply had him guessing

she'd made the trip to escape from a personal relationship. Though it clearly had nothing to do with him, he keyed the information away in his memory bank.

'We're about ten minutes out of town,' he said.

She edged forward, apparently buoyed by the news.

'Shouldn't we be seeing some lights across the hills?'

'I hope you're not expecting high-rises, coloured lights and trams similar to Melbourne.'

'Give me some credit, but I would have expected a few lights.'

'You can soon judge for yourself.'

As the vehicle reached the top of a rise, he said, 'There it is. Koala Bay at night.'

Deb blinked, and then decided if she blinked again the few lights she saw might multiply.

'This is the island's biggest town? Where is everything? Anyone?'

'It must be around eleven o'clock.

They're probably watching television, reading, in bed, take your pick. There are no nightclubs. Now, where do I drop you off?'

'I hope it's not out of your way,' she said, working to inject a touch of timidity into her voice.

He glanced across at her. She thought his eyes gleamed.

'Don't worry, I'm not planning to abandon you by the roadside.'

Was he a mind-reader? She squirmed, and denied him the pleasure of knowing he'd tapped into her mind by saying in a slightly teasing tone, 'Of course you're not. You're too much of a gentleman to do that.'

He laughed pleasantly.

'You didn't give me the name of the motel you're booked into. I hope you weren't planning to find somewhere to stay after you arrived here. That could be a bit awkward this late at night.'

She smiled, delighted to tell him she'd actually made some preparations.

'I'm booked into the Koala some-thing or other.'

'Inn or Lodge?' he countered quickly.

'You're winding me up again. There can't be two places named Koala something on the island.'

He slowed the car. The corner lights of streets shone bravely into the darkness, and a few shops appeared along a strip. She heard him draw in a long breath.

'There are no places named Koala something but there's Koala Inn and Koala Lodge. Which one?'

Her confidence took a dive. She couldn't be certain, but she wasn't going to tell him. She crossed her fingers.

'Inn, that sounds familiar. It's Koala Inn.'

'Good.'

He took a right turn and a few minutes on, pulled up outside an iron fence. In the background, one tiny light shone over the door of a house. The place looked deserted, as unlike tourist accommodation as she could imagine.

'This is it?' she said, her voice rising.

'Looks as if there aren't any people staying at the moment. But it's a comfortable place, everything supplied. I'll give you a hand in and then be on my way.'

On a score of ten, her confidence had dropped beneath the halfway point again.

'I don't get it. Why doesn't the manager live on the premises?'

'This isn't a motel. It's several self-contained units. Come on, what's holding you back? I'll walk you across to the door, see you inside.'

Under other circumstances she would have told him to be on his way now. She could make it on her own, but a little voice reminded her she might have the wrong place. Her imagination took flight. The way her luck was running, she pictured herself curled up under her jacket on the concrete doorstep, through chattering teeth counting down the hours to daybreak. She wasn't prepared to risk it.

'I hate to inconvenience you any more, but I'd appreciate that,' she said, climbing down from the car. He was already striding through the open gate towards the door over which the light shone, her backpack slung on one shoulder. Why did she always seem to be hurrying to catch up with him tonight? She quickened her step once more.

'That's odd. You said your name's Langford? The notice on the door welcomes someone called Ford.'

He shrugged, and her heart did a double flip.

What if this wasn't the place into which she'd booked?

'Perhaps they didn't hear the Lang bit,' she mumbled.

'Anyway, they've left the door open for you.'

He'd assumed they were at the right place. Why not assume the same? The name was partly right, and it was, after all, close on midnight.

'Open? That's risky, isn't it?'

'That's the way island people do business. We're trusting, honest people,' he said with a smile in his voice.

It wasn't the time to start thinking how nice he could be, but even in her state of uncertainty, it slipped into her mind.

He pushed the door ajar, stood aside for her, but she hesitated briefly. He decided to enter at the same time as she pushed herself forward. She cannoned into him, started to fall, but he reached across to her, his strong arms wrapped around her body and steadied her back on to her feet. For a moment, a brief, breathtaking moment, a sliver of excitement penetrated her dark, dark day as their eyes met. Their lips lingered only a heartbeat away.

His arms fell to his side.

'Sorry,' he mumbled. 'You OK?'

'Fine.'

She brushed her pants, anxious to hide her heated cheeks. She could feel a tickling sensation on her face. Had his bristled chin actually grazed her cheek?

After stroking the spot with a finger, it began to itch, and holding her hand to the light, she saw it had picked up a couple of hairs.

'Your lady has long hair?'

He laughed.

'Yes. Long, glossy red locks.'

Wouldn't you know it! He had a woman with hair to die for. Dashing the hairs from her hand, she remarked in a fit of pique.

'Hair loss can be quite devastating for a woman. She should do something about it.'

'A few hairs? It's not a problem. Look, you'll have to excuse me. I really have to get going.'

'Don't let me keep you. Thanks for getting me here.'

And this time it wasn't hard to sound genuine. He'd been a lifesaver, and a pretty patient one at that, and his lady of the long red locks probably had a search party out looking for him. No wonder she was losing her hair. She shrugged. She had a more pressing problem. What if Koala Inn wasn't the place she'd booked into? She yawned, lacking the energy to find out.

'Have a good holiday. Tomorrow in daylight and sunshine, you'll feel differently about the island. Don't miss a trip to the fur seals. Goodbye, Deb.'

She stood by the door, watching him stride back to his vehicle. Even from the back, even in the gloom, even with a stack of things wrestling for attention in her mind, he sent her heart into a mildly disturbing flutter. An odd, wistful feeling swept over her. Could it be because Luke Darcey's goodbye sounded so final? Was he about to disappear from her life? Nonsense. He hadn't come into it. Tomorrow he'd be no more than a hiccup in the big picture of her new life. Besides, the man had too many superior traits, and her plans didn't include men, even if they were built with the sleekness of a missile and the strength of a tank.

She stood uncertainly in the door-way, then forced her attention to her present dilemma. Did she take the risk and settle in here for the night or sleep on the doorstep? Releasing the notice sticky-taped to the door, she took it inside, switched on the light and read it.

It welcomed the Ford family, said the heater had been left on for their comfort and hoped they'd spend a happy night on the island. The name and phone number of the manager was included.

Turn off the heater when you leave. Call or ring in the morning if you need anything.

The heater wasn't on as the note said, and with a sinking feeling, Deb feared the note wasn't intended for her. But she read it again. This time more attentively. The Ford family was welcomed for September eighth and today was the ninth. Wrong name, wrong night.

The Ford family had been and gone. They must have forgotten to remove the note before they left. And as there wasn't a new note for anyone else, she could assume two things. The first that she'd come to the wrong Koala whatever, the second that the unit wasn't booked for tonight. She yawned, stretched, her tired brain refusing to operate any more. The kettle, the tray of tea, coffee and sugar sachets, a packet of biscuits, all beckoned her across to the kitchen area. Slipping off her sandals, she filled and switched on the kettle, eyed the lounge and the small fan heater.

Take the chance and crash here for tonight, a voice in her head prompted. It had the ring of very good advice. Tomorrow she'd go down to the manager's office, explain her predicament and pay for the night. Crossing to the door, she switched off the outside light, put the safety chain in place, and checked that the drapes overlapped so that any inside light wouldn't give her presence away.

She drank only half a cup of tea before wriggling into the sleeping bag she carried in her backpack. Settling down in the lounge, she was almost asleep when she remembered she had no plan to retrieve her car. But tomorrow could bring sunshine, a new perspective on life, and almost immediately, she drifted into a dream-disturbed sleep in which she kept hearing a pounding on the door.

When she answered it, Guy stood there pointing an accusing finger at her, damning her as petty and having no understanding of a man's needs. Beside him stood his new admin assistant, a self-satisfied grin on her lips.

3

Deb woke with a start. Sitting up, it became obvious the loud, insistent knocking on the door was real. Her stomach knotted. The manager had arrived to find her squatting on the premises! What on earth should she do? Uneasy, indecisive, sweating, she sprang to her feet as silently and lithely as a stalking cat and began folding her sleeping bag.

'Deb, are you in there? Come on, open up. I haven't got all day. It's Darcy . . . Luke Darcy.'

Pausing only to draw in a long breath of relief, she dashed to the door, and swung it open.

'What kept you?'

He wore a crisp blue shirt, looked beautifully scrubbed up, smelled of soap, or shaving cream, or something equally as pleasant. She glanced down at her crumpled clothes, her bare feet, and ran her hand through her hair hanging long and loose. She probably looked as she felt — a pathetic, homeless charity case.

She wanted to reach up and hug him. She couldn't believe seeing him could feel so good.

'Thank goodness it's you. I thought the manager might have caught me.'

'Caught you? Doing what, stealing the silver?'

He laughed and his eyes gleamed.

'I have no idea what you're doing here, but I'm glad to see you. I'll explain later, but can we get out of here before anyone else knocks on the door?'

'You've obviously forgotten your car's sitting back there on the highway. I'm here with my jump leads to get you back on the road on my way to work.'

She dashed her hand to her head.

'I thought of it before I drifted off last night, and I've been asleep ever since. I'm really grateful, Luke. Give me a few ticks to have a wash and brush up.'

He looked her up and down, and in the morning light she noted the blue, a deep blue, of his eyes was fringed by dark lashes. She blinked, how could she be even vaguely noting his physical attributes at this moment of crisis?

'Slept in your clothes, did you?' he asked, bringing her back to reality with a start.

Why deny the obvious?

'Too tired to change. I must look awful,' she said, as she padded into the bathroom, threw some water over her face and hands, finger-combed her hair and reset it in the scrunchie.

Forget how you look, she told her mirror image, just get out of here.

Back in the main room, as she slipped her feet into her sandals, she noticed her sleeping bag and backpack were missing. Luke had apparently already taken them out. He'd also rinsed the mug she'd used and straightened the bench.

After checking she'd left everything as she'd found it, she closed the door with a huge sigh of relief, and removed the misleading welcome notice. He was standing by his off-road vehicle, tapping his fingers on the window glass. The irony was, he couldn't have felt a more urgent need than her to get away.

'I don't know how I can repay you for this, Luke,' she said as she climbed into the car.

'No need. All part of the local service. I've also made sure you don't get any of Sandy's hair on you today.'

He smiled, and in the morning light, his smile brought some sunshine to her jaded thoughts. On another occasion it probably would have prompted her heart into a gentle flutter. But a sense of relief dominated her feelings, as the car moved off, relief and gratitude.

'You were saying?' she prompted as she settled back in the seat, the knot in her stomach easing.

'Sandy's hair.'

'So her name's Sandy. Goes with her

hair. She sounds very attractive.'

Luke glanced quickly across at her.

'I wouldn't call her attractive. Appealing's a better word. She has fabulous eyes. When she looks at me . . . well, she melts my heart. She's got me around her little finger.'

'Oh!'

Did she sound disappointed? Though it amused him, he felt a touch guilty because she didn't realise he was having her on.

'Did I say thank you before?'

She looked spent, out of gas, so to speak, and she actually sounded grateful. Last night's young woman hardly had an apologetic bone in her body. She'd been lively, determined, disinclined to admit to making a few elementary mistakes, challenging, interesting. He could only speculate that something further happened to rattle her after he dropped her off at the unit.

'So what caused your restless night?' he hinted.

She tucked herself into the seat.

'I don't remember saying I didn't sleep very well.'

'But you did sleep on the sofa, unless my eyes deceived me.'

'You don't miss much, do you?'

'Is everything all right? You sound a bit flat.'

She sounded more than a bit flat.

'I feel as if I've spun a few cycles in the tumble dryer.'

He laughed.

'So, out with it. Why were you so anxious to get away? What did you think the manager might catch you doing? Stealing the tea bags?'

He expected she'd laugh, instead she sighed.

'It's too depressing to talk about.'

'We've got all of half an hour. I'm up for it if you are, Deb.'

It felt good saying her name, as if they were friends. To tell the truth, he hadn't slept all that well himself. He kept thinking about her, remembering her disrespect for his advice, her long limbs, her luminous blue eyes. He was glad he had an excuse to see her in the morning. And then he'd cautioned himself. It was too soon to expect he could start living a normal life again. First he had to establish his new identity, feel comfortable and secure with it, consolidate the direction in which he now took his life. A woman, any woman, would get in the way, have questions, demand answers.

Deb wasn't keen to admit she'd stayed at the wrong place after the lecture he'd given her last night on coming unprepared, but today he'd arrived in such a friendly mood, she thought, what the heck. She intended to call on the unit manager as soon as she got her car back, and found a little place to rent. She shrugged.

'I guess you won't report me.'

He glanced quickly across at her, the dark lashes curled over his eyes as he frowned.

'Come on. What was the something which could have me rushing to report you?'

She took a deep breath, and rattled off the words, 'I found out I had it wrong. I wasn't booked into Koala Inn.'

A smile hovered on his lips.

'Yeah? You had yourself a freebee?'

'Not intentionally,' she snapped. 'That note on the door was written for a family who stayed the night before. I read the date.'

'But you decided to crash there anyway?'

She tilted her head.

'Naturally I intend to go see the manager and pay for the night when I get back.'

His hand left the steering wheel and touched her arm.

'Stop worrying about it. They'll understand. Mention my name if you need someone to corroborate your story.'

His reassuring touch made her feel even more wretched.

'If you're thinking I'd try something like that on purpose . . . '

'No need to get defensive. I was

thinking a guy might have to keep an eye out for you while you're on the island. You, Ms Langford, are accident-prone.'

She squirmed in her seat, his suggestion pleasing her. Having his wonderful eyes looking out for you could be her idea of Eden, but until Deb knew him a whole lot better, until she established he wasn't another selfish sod like Guy, Eden would have to wait.

'I can handle it,' she said quietly.

'I hope so. What are your plans?'

'I'll go looking for a comfortable little cottage to rent when I recover my car. Can you recommend where I should start?'

'For how long?'

'Three months.' Then she added, 'Maximum,' with emphasis.

He raised his dark brows.

'As long as that? Call into Still Waters agency in the main street. They're sure to have something for a girl with your looks.'

She tried not to blush at the thought that he could be coming on to her. She remembered Sandy, the woman he had to rush home to last night, and decided to remind him about her.

'I want to rent a cottage, not a beauty consultant's shop. You didn't tell me how you fared last night. Did you get into trouble for being late home?'

'Yeah. And it didn't go down too well when I explained I'd been hijacked on the road by a lovely young woman in a fragile mood.'

It brought a smile to her lips.

'I hope she wasn't very upset.'

'She always gives me a hard time when I'm late. I can't blame her really. She's on her own all day.'

'Doesn't she have interests of her own, a job?' she asked, thinking his Sandy sounded dull and insular, which didn't quite equate with the picture of the glossy red-head she had in her mind.

He laughed.

'Sure, digging holes, chewing bones

and chasing butterflies, but her evening walk along the beach beats that. She gets quite aggravated if she misses out.'

The sun came out. In profile, lines crinkled from the corners of his eyes, his dark lashes curled engagingly. She laughed, too.

'Ah, I get it. Sandy's your dog. And you let me think . . . you deliberately led me on. Shame on you, Mr Darcy.'

'Ms Langford, you make it easy for people to wind you up. You tend to leap to conclusions.'

'I have to plead guilty to that. It's an annoying habit of mine.'

'Recently acquired?'

'That's all I'm saying. In return, may I claim the right to a statement of honesty about you?'

He turned his head briefly, the vehicle slowed, as if he'd lost concentration.

'Ask away. I can't guarantee an answer.'

Not for the first time, it occurred to her that this man was very reluctant to talk about himself. She reminded herself that she was much the same.

'I accept I'm easily wound up these days. You, Mr Darcy, patronise women.'

He kept his eyes trained on the road, showing no emotional response.

'I hadn't noticed.'

'You should start noticing.'

She laughed.

'If you only have a dog in your life, that could be why.'

'I've got an older sister who constantly gives me a hard time about my faults. Who tells you about yours?'

Her lips curved.

'I'm thinking of getting a cat.'

'No man?'

'Not any more.'

The words were out before Deb had time to check them.

'Separated? Divorced?'

He glanced across at her.

Keep your reply simple, you can't get into discussing your split with Guy, she urged herself.

Staging a smile, she said lightly, 'Let's

just say, I'm fancy free.'

'And loving it?' he said lightly.

She smiled. She didn't really know how she felt about her unexpected single status. All she knew was she'd had a lucky escape from a man with no scruples, but the hurt lingered.

'Of course,' she said with a breezy dash of her hands before changing the subject. 'The island looks much more welcoming in the light.'

'It's a great place, even in winter. I love the sea in winter.'

Funny he should say that. In Melbourne, she lived at a beach suburb close to the city, and enjoyed her winter morning walks along the shore, the waves crashing against the rocks, the wind tugging at her hair and around the hem of her long coat. But she declined to comment, in case he thought she agreed only to impress him.

'It's going to take me a while before I forget my introduction to it. The only thing missing last night was a down-pour of rain.' Laughing, she added, 'I'll recover, of course. Actually I'm looking forward to driving around and visiting some of its special features. I believe there are koalas up every tree. How long before we get back to my car?'

'Around another bend or two.'

The sunshine through the windscreen warmed her. She felt drowsy. Her lids flickered up and down, desperate for sleep, but the minute she felt his hand on her arm, the slowing of the vehicle, she was wide awake, searching the roadside for her little hatchback. It was there. An odd feeling that she'd woken from a dream washed over her. She shook her head, her hair bouncing across her shoulders.

'Am I seeing things, or is that really my car, my ticket to freedom?'

He laughed.

'It looks real enough to me.'

'And it seems to be in one piece. Wow!'

She caught his satisfied glance.

'I always keep my promises.'

It took a couple of locks on the

steering wheel to turn his vehicle across the road and to nose in ahead of hers. She wrenched open the door and raced along to it, reaching into her pants' pocket for the keys.

Inside the car she checked to see if things were as she'd left it. Outside, Luke lifted the bonnet and began attaching the leads to the battery terminals. As he started his motor, she climbed from the car, restless to be on her way.

'How long?' she asked.

'A minute or two. Did you check for snakes?'

She jumped back from the vehicles.

'Snakes! Oh, no, I thought you were going to do that. I could have been bitten.'

'I wouldn't have let you near the car if I didn't think you were safe. The poor old snake's the one who's in danger.'

He disconnected the leads.

'Try turning over your motor. If it's a goer, I'll take a look under the car.'

'Er . . . could you try the engine? The

thought of snakes . . . '

Amusement shone in his eyes as he accepted the keys she held out to him and started the engine with the first turn.

'I'm on my way out of here,' she shouted sashaying along the verge.

He was grinning as he stepped from the car and moved towards her. Joy and relief driving her, and on her tiptoes, she planted an impetuous kiss on his cheek — and regretted it immediately.

The scent of him, the warmth, the feel of his flesh beneath her lips, signalled unambiguously that she wasn't over men, but she was over Guy.

She managed a quiet, 'You're a lifesaver,' as, uncertain, she stood beside him feeling small, physically and emotionally tied up in knots.

'You're welcome,' he said, moving aside. 'Now, would you care to observe while I check out if any snakes have taken advantage of the free accommodation and settled under the car overnight? You might have to do it by yourself some time.'

She gulped, unsure if he was also referring to the free night she'd just spent as well as the snakes.

'I'll watch from a distance this time. Maybe later I can learn the technique. I'm still trying to adjust to being on an island,' she said with a laugh and a sweep of her hair.

He tilted his head, found a stout stick on the side of the road, stripped it of saplings with a couple of swift strikes, and crouching on strong thighs poked it under the car at various angles. She backed off to watch from a comfortable distance. As he shifted position, sometimes lying flat on his back, his head disappearing beneath the car, her gaze, her emotions were trapped by his spectacular body strength. She tried to concentrate on the fact that he searched for a snake, but her mind refused to co-operate. It had only one focus — the man.

Disgusted with herself, she strolled away, saying, 'While you're doing that, I might take a look around the area where the kangaroo went into the bushes last night. Is it safe in there?'

He was on his feet, dusting at his navy trousers.

'If you go into the bushes, you could invite more trouble. Snakes enjoy sunning themselves and those sandals you're wearing aren't recommended bush wear.'

She jumped back from the verge.

'You're teasing, again.'

'A little, but it's a cardinal rule. You never go into the bush unless you're wearing sturdy shoes. It's a bit early in the season for an invasion of snakes, but you can't be too careful. Last week . . . '

'Thanks, but can we give that story a miss? I'll rely on you to talk to the Ranger about last night's little drama. Should I tie a piece of ribbon to the area to mark the spot?'

'Good idea. Have you got one?'

'My scrunchie, maybe?'

Releasing her hair, it fell loosely to her shoulders, she folded one side behind her ear, as she slipped the circle of elasticised material around a branch. 'OK, can I get out of here now?'

He stood by her car, his arm resting on the roof. 'I'd better get moving, too.'

'Today's begun so well, I'm starting to think I had all my downsides on the one day. My future looks fan-tas-magorical.' She felt fantasmagorical as she returned to her car, ready to climb in, but by now he was inspecting her tyres.

'Does that include meeting me?'

Thank goodness he didn't see the heat rise up her neck and extend into her face.

'I'd forgotten that.'

'Already, and I'm still here. I could be the invisible man.'

'Luke Darcy, I believe you're hinting for more compliments. You should quit while you're ahead.'

'I'd settle for your company at dinner once you're established. Expecting bended knees and a plea for forgiveness would be too much to ask of a woman with attitude.'

His smile lit his face.

She had no intention of being a pushover to any man, even one who had a rolled gold appearance and practical skills to enhance it. Of course the offer of dinner tempted her, but to accept would be to compromise her plans. Still it seemed ungrateful to reject his invitation coldly, so she smiled, hoping she sounded natural and said, 'That would be nice. After I've settled in I'll get back to you.'

'Fine.'

Her thanks would have to satisfy him, but somehow it didn't satisfy her.

'I don't know what I'd have done without you. You've been wonderful,' she added.

'Forget it.'

He glanced at his watch.

'I'll see you off before I leave for the ferry terminal so I'm certain your car starts.'

After he opened her door, she

climbed in. As he closed it, he said, 'Make a new battery and a torch your first two purchases when you get back to town. That way I won't receive another SOS from you. Oh, and a pair of strong, leather boots would be wise for protection against those snakes.'

He grinned. She shuddered at the thought.

'They'll have to wait until I've found a place to rent and had a shower.'

She staged a laugh, unable to think clearly through a fog of ambivalence. He didn't seem at all put out that she'd turned down his dinner invitation. All he did was hand her a brochure with the ferry terminal phone number and say in an amused tone, 'Keep this in the car in case you get into more strife. Enjoy your stay.'

'Thanks.'

Suddenly her voice became choked with tears. She revved the engine, making it thrum into life. Refusing to look back as she pulled on to the road, tears began to trickle down her cheeks.

Exasperated, she flicked them away with her finger. The last twelve hours had left her tense, tired and vulnerable, vulnerable to a man. How had that happened?

But soon her confidence began to re-emerge as she looked around her and saw the island with unclouded eyes and an open heart. The morning sun was melting the diamonds of dew on the grasslands, a party of yellow-crested cockatoos high on the limbs of a dead tree, and yet-to-be-sheared flocks of sheep grazed on pastures beyond the fringe of trees. She glanced at her watch — not much after eight. She had a full day ahead of her, and she'd need it. First stop, the Still Waters rental agency.

The minute she walked into the premises, she realised she should first have found somewhere to shower and clean up. The receptionist eyed her with distaste. Given the chance, she'd probably refer her to the cheapest caravan park on the island, but Deb wasn't giving her the chance.

'May I speak to one of your sales people, please? Mr Luke Darcy recommended you.'

'Oh, you must want to speak to Ms Crawford.'

Again the receptionist's disapproving glance swept over her.

'She's his . . . '

The remainder of the sentence was lost as she swept into an adjoining office. Deb mentally finished the it with 'his lady,' as she set back her shoulders, determined not to be even vaguely miffed. Yet, she teased herself by wondering how glamorous his lady would be.

Minutes later, a woman, perhaps of similar age to herself, strolled out wearing a tailored suit of black with a short skirt, stiletto-heeled black shoes, and understated gold ear-rings. Her fair hair was short, expertly shaped to sit behind one ear. Deb looked down at her own crumpled T-shirt and cropped pants, her sandals and cringed mentally.

Ms Crawford, with her glossie catalogue image, came towards her. Disbelieving eyes ranged over her. Deb's ready smile slipped from her eyes.

'Er . . . I'm Mandy Crawford, Miss Langford? You said Mr Darcy, Mr Luke Darcy, recommended you to us.'

'Is there another Mr Darcy on the island?'

She laughed indulgently.

'Alas, you only meet one of him in a lifetime. How can I help?'

'I'm looking for a small cottage to rent.'

'You're probably after a practical, one-bedroomed unit on the outskirts of town. We might have a little place out at . . . '

Deb couldn't blame Ms Crawford for thinking she was a pauper.

'I know I look a mess, but if you'd been . . . ' She shrugged. 'My car broke down miles out of town last night.'

'I see. You had to sleep in it?' she prompted.

'It's a long story, but the short version is, I have to find somewhere to rent, today. I'm after a cottage with a garden and a study for my work, and a view, naturally.'

Ms Crawford smiled.

'Sea views are very expensive. Luke has one, of course, but . . . '

Was Ms Crawford trying hard to impress upon her that Luke was her property, too?

'I'm sure he has, but can you show me anything along the lines I've mentioned? We can talk rents later.'

'Still Waters has a few addresses you might care to inspect. Is it convenient now?'

'I'd prefer to suss them out first and get back to you.'

She smiled.

'But you won't get to see inside unless I'm there to open up.'

Deb sighed. She must not be talked into something she didn't want because the rent was cheap. She intended this island exercise to be one of self-indulgence. For the first time, perhaps in her life, she'd decided to put herself and her own needs first. For years she'd had the rôles of confidante and peacemaker to her mother after her unfortunate second marriage to a much younger man. Once her mother walked away from the union, Guy then soaked up her independence and energy, making demands upon her social and work times, claiming privilege as her boss and her partner.

'Fine, let's go.'

As they drove down the main street, Ms Crawford said, 'So you know our man of mystery from the old days, eh? I'm dying to know more about him. I'm hoping you can fill in the details.'

Apparently Luke wasn't Ms Crawford's man. If he was, it couldn't have been a very intimate relationship if the property agent referred to him as our man of mystery. Even in their short time together, Deb had vaguely noted his reluctance to talk about himself. Now, it seemed he was a mystery even to the people of the island.

Deb couldn't help it. Her nose positively itched to find out why.

4

Deb realised Mandy Crawford thought she knew Luke a lot better than she did. She laughed.

'You mean Luke? He's a nice guy, isn't he?'

'Nice? Please, the guy's a hunk. A mysterious hunk, but that makes him even more nail-bitingly intriguing. Tell me about him. He's from the city, isn't he? Melbourne or Adelaide? I can never pin him down.'

Deb smiled.

'Perhaps he's not ready to be pinned down, Ms Crawford.'

'It's Mandy, please. Hey, you don't think . . . I mean I wasn't implying . . . '

Deb chanced a glimpse at her. Her face had turned crimson.

'You don't have to convince me.'

'But don't you think it's odd that a man like him works on the ferry? Have you noticed his hands — long, strong fingers. Wouldn't you love to . . . ' She tilted her head. 'Sorry, my mouth's running away with me. What I mean is those hands haven't done a lot of manual work.'

Deb grinned.

'I was too busy noticing his muscles, and they are built for hard work.'

'Glad I'm not the only one to notice,' the property agent said, sounding more relaxed. 'There's another puzzling thing about Luke. He never has any family or friends come visit. I mean, he lives at a tourist destination and has no visitors. No mother, father, sisters, lady friend, in fact you're the first person in six months to show up on the island who knows him. So come on, out with it, what's the gorgeous Mr Darcy been up to? I bet you know more than you're telling.'

Deb squirmed. She knew he had a sister, but only by default.

'I'm Debra, by the way. Actually I may have misled you. I only met him on the ferry coming over.'

'Wow! He made overtures to you? He didn't waste any time. Lucky you.'

'Hey, you're 'way ahead of yourself. All he did was give me a lift into town after my car broke down, and recommend your agency.'

'Just my luck. I thought I might discover more about him. He's a good-looking guy going to waste on this island.'

'Not having any luck with him, Mandy?'

'We have coffee occasionally. He changes my light bulbs. He's always very pleasant, but very private.'

'Perhaps he's having a change of scene.'

'I thought of that, but no family, no visitors? And to my knowledge he's never been across to the mainland in all the time he's been here. I'd call that more than a change. That's abandonment. It occurred to me he might be a former priest who's left his order. Can't you see him in long black priestly robes, sort of darkly brooding?'

Actually Deb could, but it didn't seem appropriate to confide that to a stranger. In fact, she felt uncomfortable, vaguely disloyal, discussing the man who'd been so helpful to her. She joked to lighten the discussion.

'You must have been reading Wuthering Heights recently.'

Mandy laughed.

'Girl talk. I hope you don't mind. There are so few eligible men on the island, one sometimes allows the imagination full rein. I did wonder about an affair of the heart. Priest falls in love, priest flees temptation, leaves his former life behind. What do you think? That's something he wouldn't want to talk about.'

Deb nodded, and decided the subject had gone far enough.

'Are we almost at one of the properties?'

They were driving up a rise alongside the sea.

'I think Honeysuckle Cottage might

appeal to you. It's around the next bend and a very reasonable rent.'

'It sounds lovely.'

Deb warned herself not to get enthusiastic before she saw the place, which was a wise reminder, for, perched high on a windswept hill overlooking the water, if not already a health and safety risk, Honeysuckle Cottage soon would be.

'Sorry,' she said. 'I couldn't afford the hospital bills if I fall through the floor boards, or the wind sweeps me up with the roof one night.'

The second place they visited had a huge, rambling garden requiring the services of a full-time gardener, and a dark house full of dusty Persian carpets. Disappointed with their progress, Deb reiterated her needs.

'Can't you show me anything in good repair that isn't surrounded by land big enough to hold a garden party?'

'Yes, but not on the seafront.'

Mandy turned the car around and they set off back to town. That's when

Deb saw it up a side street.

'Stop,' she directed and pointed. 'That place. Can we look at it?'

'It's not on the seafront, and it's got a very tiny garden.'

'But is it for rent?'

The recently-built house on a narrow block of land, sloping away from the water, was an unusual shape, but its attic-type rooms caught Deb's attention. It wasn't at all olde-worlde, or what she originally had in mind, but she could already picture herself in those upstairs rooms, looking over the tops of other houses to the sea. It would be ideal for her to work in.

'As it happens, it's available for four months. The owners have a farm on the mainland, a hundred or so miles from here. It's their holiday home, but they're abroad at the moment.'

Inspecting the inside of the house confirmed her must have feeling.

'I'll take it,' she said.

As they returned to the agency,

Mandy asked what she planned doing on the island.

'I'm a graphic artist,' she said. 'I was employed to do mostly sketches for brochures and leaflets, advertising boards, but I've always wanted to seriously try my hand at painting, watercolour in particular.'

'There are quite a few artists living on the island. As a matter of fact, I attend a small artists' group meeting in the community centre. Luke's also a member.'

Deb raised her brows, and said lightly, 'And are you interested in art or in Mr Darcy?'

'Debra, how could you?'

She laughed. When Deb first saw her in her business clothes with her chic city hair-do, she thought Mandy wasn't her type. She now conceded she actually enjoyed the agent's openness.

'Can I move into the house today? What's it called again?'

'Elanora, aboriginal for home by the sea. I guess you're keen to take a shower and clean up.'

Deb raised her brows and laughed.

'Am I so smelly?'

'Put it this way. I won't have to spray out the car, but you do look as if you've been sparring in the gym.'

As they took the road to the agency, they chatted about the island facilities, and once there Deb completed the rental agreement, paid a month's rent and closed her hand firmly around the key to Elanora.

'After you get settled, give me a ring. We could have a coffee, compare notes on the gorgeous Luke,' Mandy said.

Deb next called to settle up with the manager for last night's illegal stop-over, and having scooted in and out hoping to be noticed as little as possible, she drove back to her new house. After unpacking, showering and changing, she returned to a garage she'd noticed in the shopping strip. There, she left her car to have a new battery installed, did some shopping at the supermarket and happily idled home along the beachfront.

She located the steep flight of steps she'd noticed from the house, built into the cliffside. They led her up to the main road, and from there she began the steady climb up the road to Elanora. Glowing with vitality and warmth, she breathed the sea air with a heady sense of freedom at having only herself to please.

As she prepared a late lunch, her thoughts returned to Luke Darcy. Mandy certainly had the man on her mind, but so did she. In fact she couldn't get him out of her head. Mandy described him as a man of mystery. It tallied. From the beginning she'd wondered about him, too, noticed how he dodged personal questions. She couldn't read him well at all, but she wasn't about to make any snap judgments. She had misjudged Guy's character badly, and she'd known him longer.

Thoughts of Luke set in, and her mind searched for reasons as to why he both fascinated and interested her when she'd come here hung-up about men and determined never to let another one into her life. She decided she'd probably become hooked on the mystery, not the man. Tossing her head, she rationalised people who lived on islands loved to have a mystery to go with the presupposed notion of isolation. She wasn't even remotely interested in Luke himself — he was just another male.

Deb walked back to town late in the afternoon, dallied along the shopping strip, bought a torch and smiled as she imagined how cock-a-hoop Luke would be if he knew she hadn't dared ignore his advice. Next she called into the community centre to see if any classes interested her and took away the leaflet on the art group.

Back at the garage the mechanic smiled, his strong white teeth shining from a face streaked with oil.

'She'll be right, mate,' he said. 'The battery won't let you down again for a while, eh? But let's know if I can do anything else for you while you're here. Jason's the name.'

He put out his oily hand, then withdrew it with a grin. She returned his smile. She'd never been called mate before and it sounded welcoming.

'Thanks, Jason. If I have any more car problems, you're my man.'

'Yeah?' He sounded enthusiastic. 'You mentioned Darcy told you to come here. I reckon you could be his young lady, eh? My sister's going to be real hacked off when she learns our mystery man is taken.'

She laughed, flattered.

'You can reassure your sister, your mystery man isn't taken by me.'

'I'm reassured, too. If you're free, maybe we could go to the pub one night for dinner.'

Two invitations to dinner from attractive men on her first day! Men, she thought, opportunists, trying to ignore the ripple of pleasure inside her as she gave him the same response she'd given Luke.

'After I settle in, I'll get back to you.'

Deb drove home, mulling over the conversation. In time she might get back to Jason. Like Mandy, he, too, seemed open, honest, but his reference to Luke intrigued her more. Why? She'd leave it to the locals to enjoy their mystery. She'd come to the island to see if she could recapture her ability with graphics and turn it to art work which sold to galleries and well-heeled clients.

At the place she now called home, she set up her easel close to the attic window, facing the sea, arranging her brushes and paints on a folding table by its side. But two days after moving into Elenora, though her mind spun with ideas for painting the fabulous rock and seascapes on offer, she kept discarding any work she attempted. Would her confidence, her creativity never return?

Why did she feel so restless, so incapable of long stretches of concentration?

Give yourself time. You're still getting over the shock, she told herself.

Having discounted another day's work, she tried to relax in what had become her favourite chair. From the window she could see the sun slowly signalling the close of another day. A wasted day, she thought, working up some irritation with herself. Then she noticed a man and his dog on the steps leading down to the sand. She sat up, drew in her breath. She'd know Luke Darcy's athletic figure, his long stride, anywhere.

Wasn't that sunset crying out to be photographed? Couldn't she improvise from the picture later to create something stunning on paper? And didn't she need a stroll in the air to chase away the blues of another frustrating day? Reasons enough to tug her windproof jacket over her tracksuit, pull on a knitted cap and, camera in hand, she hurried down the slope towards the sea, mentally framing the magnificent orange ball as it disappeared towards the horizon, and then in her viewfinder, shooting it from various angles.

Soon she was on the steps leading down to the sand. Luke was no more than a silhouette casting a long shadow farther along the shore, but if she lingered, she'd meet him on his way back. Why on earth tempt fate? Well, for a start she owed him her thanks and she wanted to tell him she'd taken his advice and had a new battery installed in the car. And maybe, just maybe, he'd sneaked under her guard and begun to interest her on another level. Who was he, and what was he doing on the island?

She dug the toe of one sneaker into the damp sand at the water's edge, trying to recall whether he said he was from Adelaide or Melbourne. Actually he'd been non-committal, but he had mentioned a sister. As the wind tugged at her hair, she jammed her cap more tightly on to her head, pulled her jacket around her and decided to give up the wait, increasingly aware that in truth, she'd lingered because she wanted to see him. Pathetic! Her yesterdays had been a disaster, and now . . . it didn't bear thinking about.

She turned back, tucking her long, loose hair into the collar of her jacket, flicking the softer sand with her feet with each slow, deliberate step, trying not to remember another man, another place. She'd been warned that Guy didn't have the stamina or the inclination to commit to one woman, but smitten, she'd believed him when he told her he loved her. That was the tragedy. She'd ignored the signs, the innuendo, her questioning heart, and gloried in being the boss's lady.

The sun had disappeared now, as she'd reached the steps leading up to the road and flopped on to the bottom one to watch the lights turn on slowly around the coast. Damned if she was going to weep one more tear over Guy. Besides, it wasn't her heart but her pride that ached. She'd probably never loved him, but to be humiliated in front of your colleagues, to finally acknowledge that they'd been nudging one another and talking behind their hands — that took some forgetting.

Removing her camera from her pocket, she adjusted it for the changing light conditions and positioned herself to capture the steps on film, with the reflections of the town as it lit up in the background of the sea. She could paint it then, she thought, a hint of enthusiasm stirring in her heart.

Behind her, she heard someone, something approaching, a strange flopping sound, unfamiliar. She turned swiftly to find a large, hairy dog almost at her heels. She stepped aside, but not quickly enough, for it cannoned into her and sent her sprawling on to the sand, with a shriek, more of surprise than alarm. She fell softly, the dog careering on.

A voice called, 'Sandy, come back here. What the devil's going on?'

Deb sat up, peering into the gloom. He was gaining on her with long, deliberate strides. She'd seen him in the evening light before and his confident steps, the body, the old windproof jacket, the bounty of wind-teased black hair made her heart pulse uncertainly. Should she act indignantly or light-heartedly? She opted for the second. I mean, it was hard to be indignant when your butt was partly buried in the sand and your legs awry as you tried to get up!

'Does your dog have no respect?' she asked brightly as he reached her.

'Can I apologise for Sandy? Here.'

He tossed the dog's lead to the sand, stretched his arms to help her up, and she tucked her hands into his and came to her feet with a gentle tug and a spray of sand. His touch sent a warm glow rippling through her. Mandy's assertion that his were not the hands of a manual worker crossed her mind.

'No broken bones. You're not going to sue me? You're OK?' he asked.

Uncomfortably warm, she busied herself brushing the sand from the behind of her track pants.

'You're always asking me that.'

'And you're always having mishaps.'

Sandy came ambling back, and stood next to Luke, his swishing tail fanning the cool air.

'Can I help it if a mutt thinks she owns the beach?'

She leaned across and patted the dog.

'So I get to meet the woman in your life. Great red hair.'

He laughed.

'Yeah. She's my best mate, aren't you, girl?'

She ruffled the dog's coat.

'Nice to meet you, Sandy,' she said, adding, 'Would you care to come back for a coffee? I've found this great little place to rent and it's just across the road.'

Immediately the invitation fell from her lips, heat flooded back into her face, her stomach knotted. Curse her impulsive streak! What if he thought she was making overtures? The darkness hid her confusion, as she continued brushing the sand from her clothing, hoping, for what? That he'd refuse, of course.

'Sandy and I still have the second half of our walk around the cliffs. I give myself a hard time about leaving her all day, so we make up for it by taking a long walk at night.'

He'd refused, not directly, but she got the message. Her confidence took a dive, and she said the first thing that came into her head.

'I didn't realise you could walk around the cliffs. I haven't been in that direction yet.'

'You're welcome to join us, but you have to scramble over a few rocks, and as you're not familiar with the area and it's dark, I wouldn't advise it.'

She groaned inwardly. Heavens, he thought she'd hinted to be asked.

'As always, your advice is sound. Have a good walk, you two.'

'We could call later for that coffee.'

You're much too late. I've regained my sanity, she thought.

'Sorry, I've got a very busy evening planned.'

'Another time?' he suggested.

She shook her head.

'I'm flat out painting. That's why I'm here on the island. I really don't have time to socialise.'

It sounded a bit over the top, but she needed to say it to stay committed to her plan to keep men out of her life. Giving Sandy a final pat she turned towards the steps, but in the darkness, she stumbled on the first step, and quickly righted herself, praying he hadn't noticed. His slightly amused voice reached her in the gloom.

'You obviously didn't buy that torch I suggested.'

Turning back, she said as calmly as she could, 'Oh, but I did.'

'It's not doing any good in the drawer at home.'

'I suppose you get a lot of satisfaction from always being right.'

He came towards her, so close she could see the gleam in his eyes. He probably thought her an air-head. She needed to explain. Planting her feet firmly back on the sand she spoke quietly.

'I didn't plan to be down here so late.'

'Carry a spare torch in your jacket pocket. You never know when you're going to need it. I'll shine mine up the steps for you. We can't have you taking a serious tumble.'

His beam was already lighting the way. She raged silently against the way he continually took control, but he sounded genuinely concerned for her, and even with the handrail, the angle was steep, and it was dark.

Accepting his offer with as good grace as she could, she began the climb, only too aware that he watched from below. What was he thinking? Nuts, he probably wasn't wasting his thinking time on her.

'I've made it. Thanks,' she called back once she set foot on the top step.

The sooner he moved on the more

comfortable she'd feel.

'I forgot to ask about your house,' he shouted back.

'Elenora,' she called.

The wind snatched at his reply as it floated up to her, but it may have been something as innocuous as, 'Odd architecture.'

As she pushed into the stiff breeze up the hill to her house, she decided she simply had to forget Luke Darcy if she were to make this trip the new beginning she'd planned. Of course she had no serious desire to welcome him into her new life, but there were moments, brief interludes, when she found him compellingly attractive, when she found herself expecting, even hoping, he'd kiss her.

She groaned. It was time for positive action. Mr Darcy, she told herself, you're consigned to the trash bin. Not that he was trash like Guy. She didn't know him well enough to pass that judgment, but she could make some assumptions, and more and more she tended to agree with Mandy and Jason. Luke was a man without a past. Why did a well-educated man do manual, poorly-paid work? Where were his family and friends? Why did he never visit the mainland when it was no more than a fifty-minute ferry trip?

5

At last she was getting somewhere with her painting. Deb stood back from her work to cast a critical eye over it. She'd chosen to capture the view of the sea from her attic, with the steps and rocky outcrop, and so far had managed to interpret it in colour, in its loneliness, to give it the magical feel of freedom as it affected her.

The phone rang. Her heart leaped. Could it be Luke? Though he knew where she lived and could so easily have found out her phone number, he hadn't contacted her since the evening on the beach. These days, she alternated between thinking it was good news and not so good news. Wiping her brush on a cloth, she reached out to the handset.

'Hey, Deb, how about a quiet bite of lunch?' Mandy suggested.

'I'm in the middle of a creative

period,' she said. 'Come over tonight.'

'No can do. Art classes. Besides, my news is so hot it's burning my lips.'

Deb laughed. Mandy always had some little snippet or other to share with her at their regular coffee meetings, and she enjoyed their conversations, threaded as they were with humour and revealing stories about life on an island.

'Gossip is a cottage industry on Bamburra,' she'd said at the beginning of their friendship and they'd both laughed.

Occasionally she felt a little uncomfortable when Mandy rabbited on, but it was always well-intentioned talk, never malicious gossip. And she had no doubt the hot news would be as harmless as someone's dog having pups or the big sale schedules for the only dress shop in town. Still, it would be good to stretch her limbs.

'OK. I'm on my way.'

As she arrived at the little street café close to the real estate agency, she

found her friend had already comman-
deered a table and was already sipping
a café latte.

'I see you've already ordered. What's
new?' she asked, taking the other chair
at the small, round table and spooning
sugar into her coffee.

Mandy raised her brows.

'This is going to blow your socks off.'

'I hope it leaves the cream on my
coffee,' she jested before the gleam in
Mandy's eyes, the excitement in her
voice registered.

She sat forward in her chair.

'OK, blow my socks off.'

'Guess who had a visitor?'

'Mel Gibson's granddaughter?'

She tried to inject some levity into
the tiresome question.

'Has he got one?'

'Who knows. Get on with it.'

'We know this person. Go on, guess.'

Frustrated, Deb displayed the palms
of her hands, and said the first thing
that came into her head, 'Luke.'

Mandy looked crestfallen.

'You know already?'

Her friend had succeeded in gaining her interest one hundred per cent.

'Luke's had a visitor? Who? Do we know?'

'A woman. She's from the mainland and he didn't seem too happy to see her.'

Deb tried to laugh, to stay unmoved.

'You're incredible. How on earth do you know that?'

'Jess McPherson rents next door to Luke. This morning when she came in to pay her rent, she happened to mention she saw Luke and the woman arrive home after work last night. That's how we know she came across on the ferry. And she's definitely moved in. Jess saw her again this morning waving goodbye to him. They must have made it up.'

'Mandy, you should stop assuming things.'

Deb gripped her coffee cup in both hands, sipping the sweet liquid. Her pounding heart told her if the news was true, she didn't like it.

'Remember we decided he'd come to Bamburra because he'd had a broken romance in the city? It looks as if we were right. Not the priest bit, but the love affair. Wouldn't you know it? She's come over to reclaim him. We're going to have to write him off as a possible . . . '

'What?' Deb interrupted.

'As . . . er . . . a prospect, Deb?'

'I don't know where you got the idea I'd fallen for him. And we didn't decide he'd had an unhappy affair, you did.'

Her voice had a sharp edge. The perceptive Mandy picked it up.

'Then you're not bothered that Luke's lady has shown up?'

'Of course I'm not bothered in the way you're suggesting, by him or his visitor. If he's back with his love and that's what he wants, I couldn't be happier for him.'

She was making it up as she went, trying to ignore the discontentment stirring in her heart.

'Besides, she could be his sister. We know he's got a sister.'

'Jess didn't think she looked like a sister. Didn't you say his sister's older than he is? According to Jess the visitor looked about twenty something. We could throw him a party.'

'Excuse me?' Deb exclaimed with a frown.

'Why not? To meet and welcome her. Any excuse for a party.'

'I'd ask him first. He mightn't be too excited.'

'Deb, I can tell you're upset. There's no need to hide it. I thought he really fancied you, too. He was always asking about you, in fact he talked about you a lot.'

'He didn't fancy me. That's non-sense. I've hardly seen him. The truth is, he irritated me and I annoyed him — that's the sum of our relationship. Anyway, I still don't understand why it's such a big deal for him to have a visitor.'

'For the first time in six months?

Come on, Deb.'

'Have you forgotten I haven't had any visitors?'

'You've only been here a month, but . . .'

The corners of her mouth turned up.

'I am starting to wonder about that, too. I'm hoping you're going to come clean and tell me the full story one of these days.'

The smile slipped from her lips, as she touched Deb lightly on the arm.

'It might help you to talk about what happened back in Melbourne.'

'I don't need to talk about it. Guy was my boss. I thought I loved him. After he let me down I discovered it was my pride he'd hurt, not my heart. I'm over him, thanks to getting right away from the scene. End of story. You know, Mandy, my ability to draw and paint is starting to come back and your friendship has helped enormously.'

'And Luke's?'

'I'd hardly call it friendship. He happened along like the Good Samaritan and helped me out. He occasionally waves to me from his car.'

'Fair enough. Then you'll be interested in what the woman looks like.'

'Not particularly,' she replied, hoping to stem Mandy's eagerness.

'Jess reckons she's a stunner. Curves in all the right places, blonde, baby blue eyes.'

Deb attempted to turn what was fast becoming a conversation she didn't want to continue into a joke.

'Did your informant have binoculars trained on the house?'

Mandy responded with a wide grin.

'No. Have you got time for another coffee?'

'No, thanks. I must be off to capture the early afternoon light. I'll pay on the way out. Thanks for the hot gossip.'

After climbing into her car, she drove to the seafront, stopped the vehicle. Her head slumped on to the steering wheel. Her heart felt leaden. Until now she'd thought her irritating, inexplicable desire to know Luke better would pass in time as had her distress at losing

Guy. Guy's loss had brought anger and recriminations, unhealthy thoughts of revenge. She'd never had Luke, but the opportunity had been there to build a relationship, and she'd turned her back on it.

But, damn it, she'd picked herself up after Guy. Life was about rebounding from lost opportunities. Lifting her head, setting back her shoulders, she wound down the window of her car to breathe the sea air, to help cleanse her mind of the malaise she'd drifted into after Mandy's news. And resolute, she drove back through the main street and out along the road back to Iluka, hoping the drive would rid her of her negative feelings. She was in no mood to paint any more today.

Beyond the township, her foot hard on the accelerator, the car sped along, hurtling around the twists and turns. The speedometer climbed, the adrenalin of risk-taking flowed, excitement stirred in her stomach, until her hatchback curved widely at a bend, and skidded alarmingly on loose gravel. Her heart thumping, she summoned the courage not to brake in panic, and regaining control of the steering wheel, slowly urged the car back on the road and halted it. What a reckless fool she'd been allowing her emotions to take control. The memory of that first night when she'd almost killed a kangaroo flashed through her mind.

It prompted her to scan the road ahead, and to her right she noticed an animal lay prostrate. She jumped from the car and crossed in a rush to the still, grey form. A koala lay lifeless. She groaned, and her eyes misted. She couldn't have been responsible for its death, but at the speed she'd been driving, she could so easily have killed one of these cuddly marsupials. Now what? The animal was beyond help, but she vividly recalled Luke's urgent response the evening she told him she thought she'd struck a kangaroo.

'Did you check if it had a baby in its pouch?' he'd asked.

The koala's heavy body lay on its back, but somehow she managed to turn it, to locate its unusual rear-opening pouch and to slip her hand into it. She breathed quickly as she felt the presence of a little creature. Drawing it out, her temperature rising, she gasped. You couldn't call it pretty, but looking down at the helpless creature, her heart stirred. Around seven inches long, it had already started to grow fur. Since coming to the island she'd studied the natural wildlife and knew this youngster was almost ready to start leaving the pouch for short intervals.

Wrapping it gently in several layers of tissues, she transferred it to the pocket of her jacket, and returned slowly to her car, knowing she had only one option. She reached into her wallet for her mobile phone, and the card Luke had given her the night he rescued her. Deb didn't hesitate in tapping out his number at the ferry terminal.

If she really wanted his help, he said

in a business-like tone, he would get away as soon as he could. Anxious not to stand around and wait, she suggested she keep driving towards Iluka and they could meet along the road.

She'd almost reached the little ferry town when she saw his vehicle approaching. Soon she was in his car, showing him the tiny mammal, talking excitedly about finding it, asking how best to keep it alive.

For Luke, her phone call had come at an awkward time, but when he heard her voice, he was always going to move hell or high water to help. The sensible thing, the easy thing would have been to direct her to the nearest animal rescue shelter, but the opportunity had come to connect with her again and he wasn't about to pass it up.

These last few weeks he'd found any number of reasons — the prime one being her insistence she'd come to paint not to socialise — for not getting in touch, but it was damned hard to stay away.

'We'll go back to Iluka to the wildlife shelter there. It's the closest. They'll take it in. It'll be traumatised, but it should have a fair chance of surviving.'

He smiled as he started the vehicle.

'I bet you've already decided on a name for it.'

She laughed quietly.

'I've been calling it Sweet Pea in my mind, but I've warned myself not to get too fond of it. It's not the kind of pet you can take for a walk along the sand.'

'I hope Sweet Pea turns out to be a girl. Did you get a pet?'

'No. I'm still thinking about it.'

'Too busy painting, I guess. How's it going?'

'It's starting to happen for me, not before time.'

She sounded enthusiastic.

'You've appreciated the quietness? No interruptions?'

'I guess.'

'I'd like to see some of your work some time.'

'Mandy's arranged to hang a couple

of my watercolours in the estate agency once they've been framed.'

He hated to admit it, but being with him appeared to make her uncomfortable. Why? His first thought knotted his stomach. Could she have learned about his past? He pretended a nonchalance he didn't feel.

'You mean I have to wait to give my opinion?'

'I've heard you're pretty busy at the moment,' she said, her voice harsh.

'I can always find time for things I really want to do.'

He smiled, but he watched her toss back her hair, tilt her chin.

'Give me a call. We can organise dinner. I believe you have a guest. She'd be welcome, too.'

Anxiety settled in his stomach.

'You heard Vanessa was staying with me?'

'Is that her name? By now, the entire island's heard,' she snapped.

He forced a laugh. 'Why the great interest?'

'Bamburra's most eligible bachelor, and suddenly his ex arrives. That's news, particularly to the single woman.'

He could almost feel the coldness in her glance, the ice in those luminous blue eyes. He didn't know whether to laugh at the irony of it, or to panic that people knew of Vanessa's presence.

'Minx? Is that what they're calling her?'

'Er . . . yes, so I'm told.'

'Ah, got it. You've been talking to the town crier.'

He attempted a laugh. She tilted her head.

'Pardon?'

'Mandy,' he said, his mind racing.

He liked the woman, but she'd appointed herself his watchdog. She checked on what he'd had for dinner, if he needed any shirts ironed, all kinds of thoughtful things, but it irritated him and impinged on his privacy. And her awkward questions about his past sent shivers up his spine. Just one slip and the truth about his past could start to unravel.

He'd tried to avoid her, but she kept popping up around so many corners that sometime he felt the island was no larger than a walk-in wardrobe.

Deb shifted in her seat.

'I'm giving no names.'

'You don't have to. At the estate agency our Mandy is responsible for every story that's in circulation. But how the devil she's worked out who Vanessa is escapes me.'

When he'd spotted Vanessa on the evening ferry yesterday, he hadn't been totally surprised. There was always the possibility she'd find him but confident he held the ascendancy over her, after a chat, he thought she'd agree to return to the mainland on the first ferry trip next morning. But later she appealed to him to stay until the weekend, and against his better judgement, he agreed after she promised not to talk to anyone about their past. Obviously a giant mistake. People were already speculating about her presence. His hands gripped the steering wheel.

'Come on, Luke, do you deny you have a live-in lady, ex or not?'

'She's only a school kid.'

He heard her intake of breath.

'Really? That's not what my sources tell me.'

'Your sources are gossips, unpleasant gossips. Frankly, I wouldn't take their word for anything, and I don't understand their interest,' he growled.

'You can't blame people for wondering. After all, you're the uncrowned king of sex appeal over here. I'm told your lady is stunningly attractive and definitely not a kid,' she mocked.

The speculation about Vanessa troubled and astonished him, but already he'd started to wonder if it wouldn't be easier to go along with the gossip rather than try to deny it. Once she returned to the mainland, her visit would be shrugged off as a final attempt at a reconciliation. The less she had to explain about her presence and exodus, the happier he'd feel, the sooner things could get back to normal.

But would they? Admitting Vanessa was his lady could ruin any chance of a relationship with Deb in the future. The scent of her, the warmth of her presence, his hopes to know her better were up for grabs if he chose that path. But so, too, was his chance of putting his past behind him for ever.

He yearned to trust Deb, to tell her the whole sordid story, but once you stop trusting people, it's hard to turn your feelings around. He wasn't yet ready to reinvest his trust in anybody.

'OK, you've got me. She's very sophisticated for her age, attractive and we're trying again. Satisfied?'

Her shaky laugh confused him. Did she accept his story?

'If that's what you say.'

He drummed on the steering wheel, wishing he'd sounded more plausible, more definite.

'I can't win. I've agreed the gossips are right and you still doubt me.'

She clipped her long hair behind one ear and said breezily, 'I'm not all that interested.'

He laughed harshly.

'Why not? If the entire island has my love life under the microscope, why deny yourself the pleasure of viewing it with them?'

She tilted her head, and said heatedly, 'I said I'm not interested.'

'In case you get interested, you have my permission to confirm to everyone their suspicions are correct. Vanessa and I are . . . '

She broke in, 'So Mandy was right?'

'Mandy needs someone to take her in hand.'

'I think she hoped it might be you, but that's all gone pear-shaped for her.'

'Huh, as if . . . '

His foot touched the accelerator and the car leaped forward.

'Let's get Sweet Pea to the wild life shelter, I want to return to work.'

Deb felt disloyal. She hadn't intended to tell him Mandy was her source of information or how her friend felt about him, but he wasn't blind, he must have guessed. Had he also guessed how drawn she was to him? And why did his assertion that the woman living at his place was his love affect her? Was she fooling herself to think he hadn't sounded all that convincing? And could she believe the woman was only a school girl.

Perhaps he'd lied about her age to stoke up his reputation with women. It didn't fit with what she knew of him, either. How she hated the idea he may have lied to her, but even more she hated the idea that he'd told her the truth.

She should have felt relieved that he wasn't available — it would compel her to get over him. Instead, she felt confused, very confused. She dragged her mind back to Sweet Pea, tucked safely into her pocket. Her fingers outlined the soft contours of its body through the material of her jacket. She stroked it lightly, trying to shift her concentration from the man who sat, unmoved, in control beside her.

'Why do koalas insist on crossing roads when they have all those acres of bush available to them?' she asked, in an attempt at a normal conversation.

'They don't drink any liquid. The particular gum leaves they eat give them all the moisture they need. So when they run out of the eucalyptus in their territory, they have to go looking for a fresh supply. They can't read road signs which say, Dangerous. Slow Down. They take off whenever it suits.'

His explanation brought a brief smile to her lips.

'And they risk getting caught by cars because they're so slow and cumbersome on the ground.'

'That's a popular myth. They give the impression of being slow, lazy, sleeping their lives away, but if necessary they can be very fast on their feet. One day I'll take you out spotting them. They can really hike when they travel over land from tree to tree. But then, so, too, can the road traffic, and that often wins.'

The car slowed and turned into a driveway where a large yellow sign announced, Wild Life Shelter. At last, Deb thought, breathing more easily.

'This is it. Would you like to come in?'

She nodded.

'What are Sweet Pea's chances?'

'Who knows? It'll have to be hand-fed for sometime. Although they start leaving the pouch occasionally after six months, they're not weaned on to gum leaves for another six months.'

'So when do they start riding on their mother's back?'

He laughed easily. She loved he way he laughed, the way his eyes shone. It made her forget how angry, how disappointed she was with him.

'Cute little things, aren't they? They hitch a ride at about eight or nine months, but I'm not the expert, Janet is.

She runs the shelter. Your little mate will get the best treatment possible.'

A woman in her forties with a tanned, caring face, wearing rubber gloves and a leather apron over her dark slacks and sweater, approached down the drive to greet them as they stepped from the vehicle.

'Hello,' she called, 'how's the patient?'

Deb smiled.

'You must be Janet. I'm Deb. I'm happy to say Sweet Pea's still breathing.'

Janet pulled off one glove, tucked it in her apron pocket and reached for the tiny creature, the soft pad of her finger stroked it gently.

'Good to meet you, Deb. I've prepared a formula of milk in a syringe ready to feed Sweet Pea, did you say? Would you like to stay and watch? You could meet a couple of my other patients. By the way, we may have to christen it Peanut if we find it's a little guy.'

She laughed.

Deb was about to nod when Luke intervened.

'Another time. Unfortunately, I have to return to work after I give Deb a lift back to her car.'

He placed his hand casually on her arm and smiled.

'Like Sweet Pea, this woman has a habit of hitching a ride.'

'And it's obvious you don't mind picking her up.' Janet said, her mouth curving merrily. 'I've been wondering when you'd find yourself a pretty woman, Luke,' she added.

Tight-lipped, Deb glanced in his direction, waiting for him to deny it. His hand fell from her arm, his smile faded.

'We have to go,' he said, beating a fast retreat.

Janet seemed not to notice.

'See yourselves out, I have a baby to feed.'

As they made their way back to the car, Deb hissed, 'Why didn't you correct her? You have not found yourself a woman.'

'Does it matter? I don't want to talk about it.'

'I do. Of course it matters, or was I dreaming only minutes ago when you said you're trying to make it again with your ex? Believe me, if I was her I'd tell you to get lost, big time.'

'But you're not.'

He sounded angry, and he length-ened his stride to the driver's side of the car. She wrenched open the car door, raised her voice so he couldn't claim he didn't hear.

'You've got that right. I expect honesty from men. You seem to have given it the slip.'

Deb sat on the edge of the seat, fuming. She couldn't figure him out. What motive did he have for allowing Janet to think they were seeing one another? What motive did he have for a whole host of things he did? Yes, he had some generous qualities, but she couldn't deny the enigmatic side of his character. So much about his behaviour troubled her. And, having lived through her traumatic experience with Guy, she could no longer ignore the confused signals he sent, in the hope they'd go away.

Guy had told her to get over it or she was out of a job. She'd taken the latter option, and eventually did get over him. But now she had to get over her feelings for a man who stirred her emotions as no other man had.

She remained tense, on the edge of the seat on the journey back to her car, giving him yes and no answers to unnecessary questions, until finally they lapsed into an awkward silence. When she saw her hatchback around the next bend, she took a long relieved breath, which she wanted him to hear.

As he pulled into the side of the road, she said, 'Thank you for helping me out again. I won't bother you any more. Goodbye.'

'I'll let you know how young Sweet Pea gets on.'

'No need. I'll make my own enquiries, thanks, and I'd like to pay for the cost of your petrol. I'll put a cheque in the mail.'

She fingered her hair as she swung down from the car.

'I'll settle for lunch some time.'

She laughed mockingly.

'Pardon me?'

He kept the motor running.

'Forget it.'

'I will, depend on it.'

Stalking to her car, she refused to look back when she heard his vehicle turn and head towards the ferry terminal in a spray of loose gravel.

6

Deb tried to finish the seascape she'd started, but somehow her brush strokes didn't happen in the right places, and her colours appeared overstated. She was forced to conclude that seeing Luke again had unsettled her.

The day stretched well into the afternoon, and nothing was happening for her. Glancing at her watch she decided to take a stroll along the beach. She could safely do so without running into Luke and Sandy who usually didn't arrive for their walk until later. But once on the sand, she felt aimless. The wind off the water penetrated through her jacket, through her track suit into her bones, so she returned home.

As she closed the door and shrugged out of her jacket, she thought how wintry her life had become, how she'd soon have to reassess her stay on the island. Under the hot shower she imagined herself washing Luke Darcy out of her life, and began humming the tune from South Pacific about washing a man out of your hair, as she poured shampoo into her hand and massaged her scalp until it tingled, and her fingers ached. Was she really going to let a man drive her away from this wonderful place?

She was drying off when she thought she heard a knock on the front door. Mandy, she hoped. She could do with the company. Wrapping her hair in a towel and her body in a towelling gown, she lifted the edge of the curtain of the upstairs bathroom and looked below.

It was dark, perhaps too dark to recognise a casual caller, but she gasped as she noted the tall, familiar figure, the sleek dog on a lead. His words floated up to her.

'That's funny, Sandy, there's a light on downstairs. I hope our accident-prone friend hasn't had another mishap. Perhaps we should go around the back to check things out.'

What should she do — continue to ignore his presence or answer the door and demand to know what he wanted? The first option won out. She kept very quiet, hoping he'd leave, but her heart pulsed when she heard the sound of footsteps on the way around to the back door. Had she shut it? She breathed easier. Yes, she hadn't opened it since coming home.

Next she recalled the light was on in the sitting-room, the curtains open. Creeping down the stairs, she slid her hand around the door of the room and groped for the switch. He was pounding on the rear door, calling her name with a sense of urgency. Sandy had started barking. Her brows shot up in exasperation. If she didn't answer, the neighbours might come storming around to see what the commotion was all about. What on earth was the matter with her, anyway? Surely she had the grit to face him and tell him where to go.

Striding to the back entrance, determined not even to ask what he wanted, she switched on the outdoor light and flung open the door.

'I hope I didn't frighten you. Sandy and I were starting to get anxious when you took so long to answer.'

'I was under the shower and didn't hear you. As you can see, I'm fine.'

His glance drifted over her.

'You certainly are.'

Heat swept into her face.

'I don't want or need your concern.'

She couldn't keep the sharpness from her voice.

'I started to worry you'd had a fall or something, but I can see you're still in one piece.'

She took a long breath, tried not to focus on the body beneath her robe, and fell into the trap of asking, 'Is there some other reason for your call?'

'I want to apologise for the other day. I owe you an explanation.'

'You don't owe me anything.'

The towel began to unravel from around her hair, so she poked it back with one hand, keeping the other clutching the wrap of her robe.

'Did you hear from Janet? It's about Peanut, and he's doing well.'

'I visited yesterday, and it's Walnut. Janet and I decided he wasn't a peanut. He's a tough little critter, so we changed it. You'll be interested to know I put her straight about our relationship, too, so there'll be no more misunderstandings. If there's nothing else, I'll say good-night.'

'I'm glad you did. I've been giving myself a hard time over that for days. That's why I'm here, to explain, and to ask for your forgiveness.'

The towel flopped from her head, her damp hair tumbling down to her shoulders. She pushed the towel to the floor.

'You took your time,' she gulped.

'It's chilly out here, and you could catch cold. I'd prefer to talk inside.'

She pushed damp strands of hair

back from her face.

'The doorstep is as good a place as any to plead your case.'

He was not coming in. She wore no clothes under her robe, and no way would she sit down in that state to listen to some concocted explanation for his behaviour, even if he were prepared to beg her forgiveness on bended knees.

'I guess it'll have to wait for another time. I can't have you catching cold. You might sue me.'

She shivered. He was right, as usual. She felt cold and miserable, but damned if she'd be persuaded by a smile to let him in.

'Go home to Vanessa, Luke,' she said, closing the door before she changed her mind.

As the sound of his footsteps retreated, Deb's heart wept. He'd gone, and she had to find a way to forget him. Painting would do that.

★ ★ ★

First she told Mandy she'd be unavailable for a day or two. Next she locked herself away in the attic, answered no phone calls or the doorbell, and painted, this time in oils. The work took shape and form. The sea had a wildness, the rocky outcrop standing dark and menacing above the crashing waves. She'd never painted with such frightening intensity, but she kept on with it, transferring her hurt and pain on to canvas with every dash of the brush. Tomorrow she would finish it, and after that? She would decide whether or not to run from this situation, or to stay on the island she had grown to love and tough it out.

The phone rang as she was making a cup of coffee, and this time she answered, expecting it to be Mandy, who by now was probably organising a search party.

'Is that Deb?' a strange female voice asked.

'Yes, Debra Langford speaking.'

Perhaps another of her paintings in

the real estate agency had sold. A hint of pleasure washed over her. Her career was taking off.

'You're a friend of Leigh's?'

She frowned and replied, 'No, you must have the wrong number.'

'I have it written in his address book. Damn, did I say Leigh? I meant Luke.'

Deb's grip on the receiver tightened.

'You mean Luke Darcy? Did he ask you to ring me?'

'I prefer to call him Leigh, but who cares what I think?'

The voice sounded petulant, young. Deb's stomach churned. She thought she knew, but she asked, 'Excuse me, who is this?'

'I'm staying with Leigh . . . I mean Luke at the moment.'

Deb dragged in her breath.

'You're Vanessa, aren't you? How can I help you?'

'So you two have talked about me,' she mocked. 'And once he's got rid of me you're going to cosy up again.'

'I don't know what you mean.'

'Oh, please. You know exactly what I'm saying. It's Deb this and Deb that. It's boring, but I thought you should know exactly what he's like, and why you'd be a fool to get too involved with him.'

She sounded nasty, as the young sometimes can.

'Look, Vanessa, there's nothing going on between us. He helped me out a few times, that's all. You needn't feel jealous. I'm not interested in Luke, not even vaguely.'

At that point she should have replaced the handset, but Vanessa's voice went on.

'You're not interested in him? Do me a favour. You're no different from all the women who think he's God's gift, but believe me, he's trouble. One day you're going to thank me for warning you about him. He's lucky he's not behind bars.'

Deb gasped, but summoned the resolve to say, 'You're confused. I know you're only young . . . '

'What makes you think I'm young?' she shrilled.

Deb ignored the question.

'If you've got a problem with Luke you'll have to talk to him about it. If the two of you have any chance of making it you have to trust him.'

Trust him, she thought, as the words slipped from her lips. Trust him? How ironic that she was advising someone else to trust a man she didn't. He hadn't even given her his real name.

Vanessa's unnerving laughter sent shivers up her spine.

'You think Leigh and me are an item? Where did that sick idea come from? Him, I suppose.'

'I repeat you have nothing to be jealous about from me. Goodbye and good luck. Something tells me you're going to need it.'

As Deb pressed the phone's off key, she stared at it as if it had attacked her. Did she really have that conversation with Luke's lady? The woman sounded obsessive. It was the only thing which explained the call. And yet she didn't sound irrational, she sounded mischievous, no, it was more like malicious, desperate to blacken the name of Luke, or was it Leigh?

Her mouth felt dry. She put on the kettle, threaded the bits of conversation through her mind trying to find some pattern, make some sense of them. Taking her cup of tea upstairs she sat in her favourite chair by the window and looked out on the lights which sparkled on the dark sea.

It had a touch of fairyland, but failed to calm her pulsing heart. She'd grown unexpectedly attached to this house and to the island life, and usually this view eased away the day's tensions. But tonight her thoughts continued to drift back to Vanessa's conversation and her warning that Luke was trouble.

He was, had been almost from the start, big trouble for her heart. And now she struggled with Vanessa's claims. Perhaps Luke had told Vanessa to leave, and, rejected and jealous, she'd made the call as an act of revenge. It was a possible explanation, but she couldn't find one as easily for Vanessa's assertion that he used two names. Why? Was he in trouble with the authorities? Was that why he'd come to the island? Dear heaven, if she believed that, Vanessa had succeeded in her attempts to blacken Luke's name. She needed to discuss it with someone, and Mandy was her best friend. But though she trusted her, she had a tendency to speak first and think later.

The person to discuss it with was Luke himself. And tomorrow, that's exactly what she'd do. He had to know what Vanessa was saying about him.

Only minutes later, her doorbell rang. She hesitated about answering it. She was in no mood for visitors, but she'd been out of circulation for two days. When she opened the door, it was Luke who stood on her doorstep. She felt the colour drain from her face, and her mouth went dry.

'You?' was all she could say.

'I'm still waiting for an opportunity to apologise about the other day.'

She took a deep breath. As emotionally unsuitable as the time was for her, she may not get another to speak to him about Vanessa. She stepped aside.

'Now's as good a time as any for us to talk.'

A sense of relief eased Luke's frustration. He'd begun to think he might never get to explain why he'd let Janet think they were an item. Fact was at the time he didn't understand why he did it himself, and the last couple of days the question had eaten away at him, made him indecisive, careless on the job. He had to put things right. He'd tried on his way home from work both days, but she hadn't answered the door. At least tonight he'd made it inside.

'Coffee?' she asked.

He felt uncomfortably aware she was working up to something.

'Thanks,' he said, 'perhaps later.'

She led him through to the little

sitting-room, indicated a comfortable chair and took one opposite him. She folded her arms across her chest, tilted her chin.

'The floor's yours. What do you have to say, Leigh?'

He started forward in his chair, sweating.

'Excuse me? Did you call me Leigh?'

She nodded, her expression inscrutable.

'By your reaction it seems Leigh is your real name.'

He slumped back into the chair.

'It's my family name. My mates call me Luke.'

'What mates? You don't have any mates.'

'I do, on the mainland. It started at school. I knocked around with three other kids, Matt, Mark and John so Leigh became Luke as in the four disciples. We masqueraded collectively as The Saints.'

He tried to laugh, but it sounded hollow.

'And you prefer Luke?'

'Yeah. I can't get the family out of the habit of calling me Leigh. So how did you find out?'

Her brows raised slightly.

'Vanessa.'

It was the answer he dreaded. Alarm gripped him. What the devil was that little witch up to after she'd promised not to make trouble if he let her stay? He should have known he couldn't trust her.

'You talked to her?'

'Come on, you know she phoned me, that's why you're here, to try to explain things, but you're wasting your time.'

Vanessa phoned Deb? Beads of sweat broke out on his forehead, his hands felt uncomfortably damp.

'I haven't been home. I came straight from work, otherwise I'd have Sandy with me.'

'OK, you didn't know. That doesn't change anything. Vanessa rang me.'

'You and Vanessa had a chat? What did you think of her?'

He thought he already knew. The distaste in Deb's voice, the coldness in her blue eyes said it.

'Put it this way. She and her conversation were very forgettable.'

It became urgent to know exactly what Vanessa said.

'I'm sorry. If I'd known she intended to contact you . . . '

'I'm still wondering why.'

'It's obvious. She wanted to make mischief between us.'

'How can you say that? There is no us. There never was, Luke.'

He moved to her side, looking down at her.

'But there was always going to be, from day one. You can't deny that. I fell for you almost from the minute I met you.'

He reached out to her, but she shrugged him off.

'You've got a great imagination. I suppose that's why you misled Janet.'

'It's been on my conscience ever since. That's the reason for my call tonight. I was stupid. Now, it seems I have to apologise for Vanessa, too. She obviously said something to upset you. What was it?'

Her facial muscles tightened.

'I'm tired of excuses and apologies. I have nothing further to say to you.'

He took a step forward, gripping her arms.

'But I have a lot I need to say to you. Primarily, you should know Vanessa isn't my lady.'

The breath of her mocking laughter feathered over him.

'She was the other day, she's not now. I wonder how you'll feel tomorrow.'

'I swear it. She is not my girlfriend. Earlier, I only agreed because it seemed easier to confirm what the islanders wanted to believe than to bother explaining. Why should I answer to them? My visitors are my business. Am I wrong?'

She tilted her head.

'Put that way . . . '

'I was really ticked off when you told

me how much interest Vanessa's arrival created. Wouldn't you be?'

She nodded.

'So you decided to string us along for a while. I guess it's not a hanging offence, but you could have trusted me. I'm not an islander.'

He smiled, easier in his mind.

'You seemed pretty interested when you questioned me.'

'To be honest, your explanation didn't sound all that convincing either, and excuse me — a school girl? That particularly didn't ring true. But why would I argue with you? If you'd been honest with me, maybe I could have been persuaded to go along with you and mislead the town gossips for a bit.'

'I wanted desperately to confide in you, but it's hard for me to trust people. When you're so used to looking over your shoulder all the time, well, it becomes a habit. I have a feeling you find it hard to trust people, too. I sense you've had a life-changing experience.'

She eased from his hold, her eyes clouded.

'Am I so transparent?'

'Not to the average person.'

'And you're not average?' she answered quickly.

'That's for you to judge. You're certainly not average, Deb. You're strong and you have attitude. I like that in a woman, but when we first met, you gave yourself away every time men were mentioned.'

'How?'

'Your voice took on a cynical tone, your eyes shadowed. I didn't need to be a rocket scientist to work out you'd come to the island to forget a man.'

He shifted his weight from one leg to the other, warned himself not to get impatient.

'Besides, a woman with your looks and figure would have had her pick of men. I figured you fell for the wrong one and he did more than walk out on you.'

Colour swept into her cheeks.

'Can we sit down? Can you bring yourself to confide in me?' he dared, sensing her uncertainty.

'Coffee,' she asked, as if to put off her decision.

'Later. Let's talk now,' he prompted.

'What have I got to lose?' she said quietly.

He placed his arm around her shoulder as they walked to the sofa and sat down side by side. Breathing easier, he assumed Vanessa hadn't told her anything mind-blowing, and he'd have his chance to retrieve the situation. Even at a time like this, when so many challenges jostled for attention in his head, he thought her beautiful, her eyes incredibly revealing, her body movements elegant, economic.

Sitting, she edged away from him, surprising him with her question.

'You didn't say why you let Janet go on thinking we were seeing one another.'

He shrugged.

'Honestly? I still haven't made sense

of how I reacted, I can only put it down to wishful thinking. I've wanted us to be together since I met you. After misleading you about Vanessa, you're probably going to find that hard to process, but it's the truth.'

He placed a finger under her chin, urging her to look at him.

'And here's another confession. I'm sorry I didn't say so immediately. Vanessa is my niece.'

She turned wide blue eyes upon him.

'Your niece?'

'Yes.'

'Why on earth didn't you say so in the beginning? It would have saved a lot of grief.'

This was where he had to tread a risky path. He wished he could open up to her, to tell her all, but to do so would be to involve other people. He answered with the phrases he'd rehearsed on his way here, hoping to satisfy her for the time being.

145

7

He began slowly. 'Why? Because Vanessa's arrival threw me. At first, I hoped to ship her back to the mainland without her presence being noted. And then you ambushed me with the information that the whole island knew about her arrival. It irritated me. I thought, let them think what they choose. You know the rest, except I didn't invite her and I don't want her here.'

'But if she's your niece . . . '

He laced his hands, put them to his chin.

'She's only seventeen, but the fact is she's totally out of control.'

'Is she ill or something? I got the impression she was a bit obsessive.'

He laughed mockingly.

'She's certainly got a sick imagination. She gets her kicks from causing trouble, particularly for me. It's probably not all her fault. She's my sister's only child, and she's been spoiled rotten.'

'Kids can rebel. I probably did a few rash things as a teenager.' She smiled. 'Stop worrying. It'll pass.'

'I doubt it. She enjoys hurting people, particularly those closest to her. My bet is she rang you to get at me. I don't know what she said, but I bet she's waiting at home to taunt me the minute I step in the door. I can't wait for her to leave at the weekend.'

'She said some very unpleasant things about you. She accused you of being a womaniser and a troublemaker.'

Her pause suggested she'd reworked the last statement. His body tensed, wracked with uncertainty.

'And you believed her?' he asked, his voice dropping to a harsh demand.

Deb's heart slowed with confusion. She felt exposed to his presence, to the overwhelming need to believe him, to be with him, but her experience with

Guy still haunted and troubled her. It was time for a reality check.

'Believe her? I'd prefer not to but what am I supposed to think? You've misled me on more than one occasion by your own admission. A man cheated on me and robbed me of my trust, and now I feel as if it's happening again. Luke, how can you ask me to trust you?' she said in little more than a murmur, her eyes misty.

Biting on her bottom lip to ward off the tears, she cursed her weakness and her indecision. Why didn't she tell him to get out of her life? Why couldn't she control this longing for him, when she knew it might lead to more pain and humiliation.

Luke reached across, his strong fingers folded around hers. With that simple action she had her answer. She wanted him. For now, she would stop fighting with herself and see what happened. Her hand still tucked in his, she looked up at him with tear-glazed eyes.

'Please make me believe you. I want to believe you.'

'There are things I've kept to myself, but I'd never knowingly hurt you,' he said quietly. 'You've come to mean everything to me.'

Her heart missed a beat.

'Do you really mean it?'

'Yes. Maybe I'm moving too fast, but you're in my thoughts day and night. My work's suffering. Tell me I have a chance.'

Afraid her emotions might run out of control, she said quietly, 'I still have something to resolve before I can move on.'

'What happened back in the city, Deb?'

In her heart, she'd already accepted his explanations about his name and Vanessa's identity. And now, she accepted his feelings for her were genuine. The other things faded into the background. Luke had none of the ugly traits demonstrated by the crowd she'd worked with at the graphics agency.

He'd put himself out to help her on several occasions, and had shown compassion to animals. Through him she'd overcome her hostility towards all men. And he held her hand now as if he cared, truly cared about her. An inner calm drifted through her body. If she told him everything, he would listen and understand.

'I thought I was over it.'

'Tell me,' he said gently. 'It can only help.'

She began slowly, the memories still imprinted like tabloid headlines in her mind.

'After coming here, I thought I had my life back together, but it's become clear I'll never rid myself completely of the demeaning experience until I open up to someone. Guy was my boss, creative beyond belief, ambitious, high on his success in business and with women, as I found out later. I went straight from university into the sophisticated world of advertising and thought I knew it all. Guy asked me out and I fell instantly and madly in love. What I didn't know, but every senior male at the office did was that he routinely romanced most of his new, young employees. It was a game he played with his boot-licking executive male staff. They placed bets on how long it would last before the woman found out. I was so naïve, so inexperienced. I thought he meant everything he said.'

She eased her hand from his hold, put both hands up to cover her face.

'What a damned fool the man was, not to recognise what he had in you.'

As she relaxed her hands, for a brief moment their eyes connected, and in his she read sincerity, affection, love. It warmed her, almost moved her to tears, but she had to go on, to bring closure to her traumatic experience. Tossing back her hair in a defiant gesture, she laced her fingers tightly in her lap, resolved not to keep anything back.

'I haven't told you the most painful part. I breezed into his office earlier than usual one morning to announce

I'd arranged an anniversary dinner as we'd been going out for six months. He'd even hinted about an engagement. I discovered him pawing his newest member of staff — a very pretty, very young admin officer. His advances were obviously welcome. I told her to leave, I'd handle it. He laughed in my face. Can you imagine how I felt? No apology, not even a tinge of regret or embarrassment. All he said was, 'You took your time finding out.' Then he told me about the standing bet, told me to deal with it, or . . . '

She stopped, and drew a breath before continuing.

' . . . or get out of his company. Not that I would have chosen any other option, but the shock, the humiliation, I can't begin to describe the emotional roller-coaster I've been on. It's taken what seems like for ever to stop hurting.'

Deb's taut body relaxed, a wave of relief swept over her.

A slow smile developed in his eyes as

he said, 'Thank goodness, I can see you're feeling better already. It's in your beautiful face.'

'Yes, but the sound of the men laughing behind my back is still there. Perhaps it might never go.'

He placed his arm around her, drew her close.

'Let me help make it go. Think of the experience as sending you to Bamburra, and to me.'

His warmth, his presence stirred her. She looked up, smiled.

'But, hey, I have to say our beginning wasn't too impressive. When I met you, I thought you were just another supercilious male with muscles.'

He cupped her chin in his hand.

'And I thought I'd met a stunning-looking woman with attitude.'

'You're exaggerating. I looked a mess that night, and I was certainly very ratty with you,' she responded, impulsively putting her lips to his cheek.

'Is that the best you can do?'

Her heart fluttered with happiness as

he kissed her lightly.

'Sure you were ratty, but the minute I saw you I thought you were beautiful. As a matter of fact, your attitude, the way you swept back your hair and glared, turned me on.'

Pleasure heated her cheeks, as she clipped her hair back over one ear without thinking.

'Thanks. I might have to keep you around. You're good for my ego. My experience sapped away my creative ability, and affected the quality of my work. Now I'm getting it back. For weeks I wandered around in a daze trying to decide what to do, how to handle things.'

He lifted her hand. His lips dropped kisses along her arm.

'Some people will do anything to get on in their jobs. Those guys weren't laughing at you, they were laughing to impress the contemptible louse who wrote their pay cheques. They were probably jealous of you, too. I bet you have more talent in your little finger than most of them have in their tiny little brains.'

'You seem to know how these things operate.'

'I'm a man, and I've had some corporate experience.'

'You really think I'm talented?' she asked, gazing up at him.

'I know so. I bought one of your seascapes from the estate agency.'

'Really?'

'Mandy promised not to tell you the name of the buyer. I think your long, hard journey has led you to a new life, a new career, and a new man.'

Holding her, his lips found hers, and captive to his kiss, she twined her arms about his neck and surrendered into his arms.

'It's what I want more than any-thing,' she whispered, 'but can we take it slowly? Last time I fell in love within seconds. This time I'd like to enjoy the experience.'

Deb's heart had no doubts — she loved him, but she had to be one hundred per cent sure they were meant to be together for all time. Since Guy she'd vowed never again to listen only to her heart. It would be hard, but she'd force herself to tread carefully, and if necessary to listen to her head.

Luke smiled down at her.

'It's a lovely idea.'

It was, but a wave of uneasiness rifled through him. He'd let his feelings, his need to have her in his life, force the pace. He'd moved too quickly for comfort, forgetting temporarily he had serious problems in his past which he didn't quite know how to deal with. He thought by coming to the island he'd found a solution, but he knew now that your past had a way of catching up with you.

'I still haven't cooked you dinner. Come tomorrow night?' she suggested, tossing her head, a hard-to-resist gleam in her eyes.

'I thought we were taking it slowly.'

'I just thought . . . '

'Why don't we start by going out to

dinner at the Seaview Hotel on Saturday night? Candlelight, soft music, wine. Let me romance you. Let me run my hand through your hair, hold you, as we dance.'

But let me get Vanessa off the island first, he added silently to himself.

He hated the idea of postponing the evening for even one night, but so much depended on driving Vanessa out of his life. She'd rung Deb, in one of her vindictive moods, she could contact her again and tell her why he came to Bamburra. That would erode the progress he'd made in establishing his new life, in winning the woman he found so beautiful.

'You're a romantic,' she said, her eyes shining.

'There's a lot you don't know about me.'

He spoke without thinking, but as the words fell out, the truth of it hit him and guilt weighed heavily on his mind.

'I'm looking forward to knowing every single thing there is to know about you. This may sound odd, but I'd like to meet Vanessa. I mean, she is your family. I don't understand it, but I think she sees me as a threat, and I'd like to reassure her I'm not. It could help your relationship with her, too. Who knows, we might be able to help her get her act together.'

He eased away from her, shook his head.

'That's not a good idea. I'm not going to expose you to her nasty tongue.'

'But she's only a kid. I can handle it. Come on, Luke, give her a chance. All she probably needs is understanding.'

Understanding? The thought reverberated in his head. How much understanding was too much? He tilted her chin with his hand.

'Deb, you're very thoughtful and sweet, but you're going to have to trust me on this. You don't want to know her.'

'Will you tell her about us?' she asked quietly.

He shifted uneasily.

'I'll have to think about it. Now, I hate to leave, but Sandy will be waiting for his walk.'

She tucked her arm into his, walked to the door by his side.

'Am I going to have to play second fiddle to Sandy?' she said lightly.

'He thinks I'm Number One. Do you?' he jested.

'You'll have to stick around and find out.'

'That will be a pleasure, Ms Langford. I'll call you soon.'

As she closed the door, he strode down the path, uncertain whether he could permit himself to feel on top of the world or if he should wait until he had Vanessa safely back on the mainland.

On Saturday morning, excitement rippled through. Tonight she had her first date with Luke. She'd packed only casual and sports clothes for the island, but Mandy had loaned her a lovely little black number.

Deb had hugged her.

'I had to apologise to Luke for speculating that his visitor was his ex, by the way,' Mandy said. 'In future if you catch me gossiping, I'll give you fifty per cent off your rental. Deal?'

'Deal,' Deb said with a smile, giving her friend a hug.

'Did you meet the niece, by the way?'

Deb had decided to tell no-one about Vanessa's unpleasant phone call. She guessed Luke would prefer it that way. No need for the island to know the girl's history, particularly as she was leaving.

'No. I gather she's been a bit of a handful and Luke's insisted she go back to live with her mother. Word is . . . '

'Is this something I might claim my fifty per cent cut on?' Deb had interrupted with a grin.

'If you don't want to know she's booked on Friday afternoon's ferry, I won't tell you,' Mandy had said with a mischievous curve of her lips.

Deb smiled now as she thought

about their conversation. Mandy's curiosity was probably incurable.

Sipping the last of her coffee, she planned the accessories to compliment Mandy's black dress. She'd wear her black strappy sandals, her gold bracelet and pendant earrings, a gift from her late father. She'd sweep her hair up at the back, tendrils curling at her neck. As she went to the bedroom to try the effect in the mirror, she spotted the postman coming up the hill on his scooter. Today he dropped a letter in her mail box. She'd been expecting a payment from the bank, so she hurried down to collect it.

As she retrieved the letter, she observed the local stamp and knew it hadn't come from the mainland. She slipped her index finger under the edge and urged the envelope open. A newspaper cutting fell to the ground. It must be a copy of the recent interview she'd given to the local paper about her coming exhibition.

How nice of them to send it, she

thought, as she bent to retrieve it.

On closer inspection, she saw the clipping came from the financial pages of a daily mainland newspaper. As she scanned its contents, her eyes blurred. She shut them tightly, hoping she was dreaming, but on re-opening them, bringing the cutting closer, its headline was unmistakable.

Bank Boss Accused of Theft, she read silently as her gaze moved to the first paragraph. *Today, Southfield Banks announced that Mr Leigh Darcy, former Director, Loans Management at head office, has resigned. This newspaper believes his resignation came in unusual circumstances after he was questioned in connection with the bank's loss of a sum of money. No charges were laid. It has been alleged that the amount of money stolen was repaid to the bank by Mr Darcy.*

The story ran on, giving details of Mr Leigh Darcy's spectacular career rise and fall in banking circles, but Deb homed in on the reproduced business portrait of the man. His hair was business-demanded short back and sides, he wore a dark suit, collar and tie, but the handsome, square-jawed face, the tilt of his head, the dark eyes which hinted at arrogance, unmistakably belonged to Luke Darcy.

Luke Darcy was Leigh Darcy, bank cheat.

She scrunched the clipping with trembling fingers, and clutching the ball of paper in her hand ran into the house, where she threw herself into a chair and damned him for being no different from all the other lying, cheating males she'd had the misfortune to meet.

8

A fire blazed inside Deb. There was only one way to put it out. Just then, the doorbell rang. Her heart quickened as she called from the upstairs window, 'Come in, the door's open. I'm nearly ready.'

She listened for the door to shut, for his footsteps to cross from the hall into the sitting room before she took several deep breaths and prepared herself. She once thought that following her final confrontation with Guy she'd had her worst life experience. Not anymore. It was about to take place.

Setting back her shoulders, she walked slowly down the stairs. Luke must have heard her and emerged from the sitting-room when she'd reached the halfway mark. He whistled.

'You look beautiful. I've never seen you looking so incredibly lovely.'

'You're such a liar,' she said evenly.

He, of course, thought she jested. He waited at the foot of the stairs, put out his hand to her. She ignored it, but smiled. The smile was always going to let her down. How could you pretend happiness when inside you burned with rage?

'Deb, what's wrong? You've gone pale. Bad news?'

'The worst news,' she said, a tremor in her voice. 'Can we go into the sitting-room?'

Brushing him aside she stalked ahead.

'Tell me what it is. Let me help. Has that sleazy fellow been worrying you again?'

'As it happens,' she said sitting down, 'you can help. Would you mind pouring me a brandy?'

He raised his brows but asked only, 'With soda?'

'Neat.'

It took every ounce of strength and determination to keep her shoulders

165

back, her head high. She'd make him sweat before she ambushed him with what she knew.

The sound of the drink spilling into the glass cut into the silence. He handed it to her. 'You should have one yourself,' she said. 'You're going to need it.'

'I'll pass. What's this all about? You mentioned bad news.'

His voice revealed his anxiety. She couldn't go on much longer without succumbing to her delicate emotional state, but she tried one more stalling tactic, hoping to make him sweat a little more.

'You sound anxious. Why don't you have that drink, and sit down?'

'Stop playing mind games and tell me what this is all about.'

'Did Vanessa get away as you planned?'

'Er . . . yes. Does this have something to do with her?'

She took a long drink from the glass, ran her tongue along her lips.

'It could have. You never did tell me what brought you to Bamburra. You've always been vague about it, but this time, I want the full, unedited story, not a version of it.'

Luke knew instinctively that somehow the unthinkable had happened and Deb knew the truth.

'I've got a bad feeling I'm going to need that drink.'

In painful silence he poured the amber fluid into a glass, took two healthy gulps and groaning, sank into a chair.

'You know about the bank theft, don't you?'

She nodded.

'How?'

'I received a newspaper cutting in the mail, but shouldn't you be telling me why you did it, why you didn't have the nerve to tell me, why you think you can run away from your crime. You're spineless. You're a deceiving, spineless . . . Dear heaven I can't believe you lied to me so callously.'

He let her go on, hearing only snatches of her denunciation as he tried to collect his thoughts, to decide where to go from here. But there was only one answer for him, one way to go. He loved Deb. More than anything he wanted to share his life with her. If only he'd had the guts to trust her earlier. But if she were the woman he thought she was, she'd give him a fair hearing, understand what he'd done, and his motive.

He eased forward in the chair, his weight on his thighs, the almost empty glass in one hand.

'Deb, I was protecting my sister. She raised me after our parents died. I owed her.'

'You don't expect me to believe you stole the money for your sister.'

'Vanessa stole the money.'

'When in a fix, blame the niece. That's always your strategy, and it's becoming a bit ho-hum.'

The mocking fury in Deb's voice knifed into him.

'It's true. Vanessa landed me in a real

mess from which there was only one exit, and I took it. I need you to understand the fragile relationship existing between the three of us. Please, listen before you judge me.'

He spread his arms, his open palms in appeal.

'I'm giving you ten minutes. After that, you're out of here.'

'Vanessa grew up resenting the special relationship I had with her mother, my sister, Meg. She blamed me when she and her mother clashed, as they often did, and frequently accused Meg of loving me more than her, which was nonsense. Meg idolised her child. Life in our household developed into one big argument. It came to a head when my niece rejected a university place, and walked out. After she'd spent her bank balance, she finished up living on the streets. Meg freaked out when she found out, so I went looking for her and brought her home. My sister begged me to get her a job at the bank.'

He shrugged, and laughed cynically.

'I always knew it was dicey, but I owed my sister big time, so I found Vanessa a clerical position and to our surprise, she settled down and seemed to be doing well.'

Deb leaned forward in her seat.

When she said, 'What went wrong?' her voice had lost its abrasive edge.

'Everything. When the manager of her division came to me with a report of missing money, not a large sum, my gut feeling was Vanessa had taken it, and private investigations confirmed my suspicions. She openly admitted it to me, almost boasted about it, said she held the winning hand, taunted me about losing my standing in the bank, and how her mother would feel if she found out. I insisted she resign so she'd be out of the way when it became public.'

'I don't follow. If she was such an irresponsible tearaway, surely it would have been better for her to face up to what she'd done.'

'I agree, for her it would have been

better, but not for my sister. Meg has high blood pressure. If she'd known, it could have killed her. I had to prevent her from finding out, and Vanessa knew that's how I'd react.'

'You're painting an awfully dark picture. It's hard to believe a young woman could be so calculating.'

'I didn't meet her father and Meg didn't tell me who he was, but my niece must have inherited his cunning. My sister is gentle, generous, loving.'

He paused there, the emotion of the moment catching in his throat. He cleared it before going on.

'The upshot was, I admitted to taking the money and pleaded a gambling addiction. Because of my track record with the bank, they agreed not to charge me if I repaid the money and resigned. Vanessa laughed when she told me she leaked the story to the financial media. The publicity left me one choice — to leave the city and take on a new identity. That's the answer to why I came to Bamburra.'

'You did all that for your sister?' Deb asked, standing up, coming to his side. 'You must love her a great deal.'

'Love, admire, respect — and more. She was twenty when we were left alone, I was eight, and would have finished up in a foster home if she hadn't insisted on keeping me with her after our parents died in a road accident. At the time, she was going with a young man who walked out on her when she told him she planned to raise me. I'd have done anything to shield her from knowing the ugly truth about her daughter. Had I not taken responsibility for the theft, the offence would have been traced back to Vanessa almost immediately. She's a very clever manipulator, but a lousy book-keeper.'

He spread his hands.

'That's it, Deb. That's what I've been hiding all these months. And I can't describe the enormous sense of relief I'm feeling right now. Thank goodness, I've told you.'

She took the glass form his hand and

placed it on the table.

'Why didn't you tell me earlier?'

'I wanted to. I've been close to telling you on several occasions, but I ran out of trust a while ago. You see, I couldn't have found a job, made a new life for myself if people thought I was crooked, so I kept my past locked away inside. And with it, my ability to trust anyone.'

He stood up, placed his hands about her arms, his eyes anxious.

'You believe me, don't you? I couldn't take it if you think I'm lying.'

Deb's confused thoughts had cleared, and everything he'd said fell into place. She'd spoken to his niece, recoiled at the spitefulness with which the girl had condemned Luke. And for the first time, his reason for coming to the island, his solitary lifestyle, his guarded answers, all had credible explanations. He was no longer the man without a past, indeed he'd become a man with an heroic past. Her heart leaped. She wanted to hold him, comfort him, love him, but it was far too early to give way to these emotions. There were matters still to be sorted between them.

'Do you trust me now, or did you only tell me this because you were forced to?'

'I'm desperately sorry. I lied to you about Vanessa being my lady, but withheld the rest in case it ruined my chances to stay on the island. I love this beautiful place, enjoy my outdoor work, the people. If they knew about my past . . . '

'Do they have to know?' she murmured.

'That's up to you. It's your decision. Am I Luke or Leigh?'

His fingers tightened around her bare arms.

'First, I need to know how you plan to handle Vanessa.'

'Yesterday I took her across to the mainland, put expenses in her pocket and watched her fly off to Queensland. I threatened if she doesn't straighten out her life I won't hesitate this time. I'll inform her mother and the police.'

'Luke, I'm not going to tell anyone, but I do think your sister should know the facts. She thinks you've gone off the rails. Have you ever thought she might blame herself for that? After all, she raised you.'

'But that means learning the truth about Vanessa.'

'It may not be such a big surprise to her. She obviously knows her daughter isn't a saint, and deep down she's probably questioning what happened. Tell her, Luke. We can be there for her, help her through the bad times. Chances are, in a few years, Vanessa will have matured and stopped thinking the world owes her a living.'

'We?' he said, drawing her close. 'Did you say we?'

She laced her fingers around his neck, and replied with a long kiss.

'Will you marry a man with a questionable past?'

'I thought we'd decided to go slowly,' she said teasingly.

'But I nearly lost you today. I can't

risk that happening again.'

'So there's more I don't know about your past?'

'A lot more, and all of it dull. Until you walked into my life, I was going steady with my work. First in the banking world and then by burying myself in the world of ferries and furry animals. I'd forgotten how good it was to be warm and intimate with someone you love.'

'I'll marry you on one condition — we start romancing as of now.'

'Sweetheart, you mean, you're up to dining out?'

'I went to a great deal of trouble to dress for tonight. I can't let that go to waste.'

'Why don't we re-run the start to the night? You go back upstairs and I'll knock on the door. That way it'll have a freshness, open up a whole new beginning, no strings attached, no baggage.'

'What a crazy idea,' she said, making for the stairs with a smile.

The doorbell sounded. Freeing her hair so that it tumbled below her shoulders, she plumped it with her hand before checking her make-up. As she began down the stairs, he was already gazing up at her, waiting for her. At the bottom step he folded her in his arms. Warm and safe, she had finally found a man she could love unconditionally. Luke's life had been crowded with nightmares, but now, the dream he'd allowed himself to dream occasionally became a rainbow with promise of sunshine after the rain.

THE END

We do hope that you have enjoyed reading this large print book.

Did you know that all of our titles are available for purchase?

We publish a wide range of high quality large print books including:
Romances, Mysteries, Classics
General Fiction
Non Fiction and Westerns

Special interest titles available in large print are:
The Little Oxford Dictionary
Music Book, Song Book
Hymn Book, Service Book

Also available from us courtesy of Oxford University Press:
Young Readers' Dictionary
(large print edition)
Young Readers' Thesaurus
(large print edition)

For further information or a free brochure, please contact us at:
Ulverscroft Large Print Books Ltd.,
The Green, Bradgate Road, Anstey,
Leicester, LE7 7FU, England.
Tel: (00 44) **0116 236 4325**
Fax: (00 44) **0116 234 0205**